WALK OF SHAME 2ND GENERATION BOOK TWO

VICTORIA ASHLEY

Styx
Copyright © 2016 Victoria Ashley

Cover Artist:
CT Cover Creations

Cover Model:
Dylan Horsch

Photographer:
Furious Fotog

Interior Design & Formatting:
Christine Borgford, Perfectly Publishable

STYX

THE NIGHT IS ALMOST OVER, but the club is packed to the brim with screaming women, waiting to get every single penny's worth of their cover charge for the night.

I don't think I've ever danced so much in the whole time that I've been working at *Walk Of Shame*. It's fucking insane tonight and to be honest; I can't wait to be out of here so I can think straight.

"Over here, Styx!"

"Bring your sexy ass to us and take it off!"

"Huuuurrryyy! Now!"

A group of women over in the VIP lounge, wave their money at me and whistle for me to come over to the couch as if I'm their little pet.

I've gotten used to it, but sometimes it makes me wish that I could go one damn night without all the screaming, whistling and groping.

I can't even count how many times my cock has been groped

and pulled on in the year that I've been here.

Lowering my jeans down my waist a bit, I straddle the lap of the closest woman in my reach and grind my hips against her, while gripping her hair, like I would if we were actually fucking.

Hands reach into my jeans, tugging in between our bodies, and fighting to shove money inside as close to my dick as they can.

One even shoves her hand in far enough to almost grab my balls.

This has me standing up from the first woman's lap and picking this new girl upside down to grind my crotch in her face.

She wants to grab my shit, then I'll pound her face with it and give her a taste of what she won't be getting tonight.

Squirming in my arms, she grabs onto my thighs and laughs as I gently bite her leg, before turning her around and setting her back on her feet.

Smiling, she places a twenty between her teeth and then bends down in front of me to shove it into the top of my jeans.

Hands grope at my ass and squeeze, my jeans immediately being ripped away, when I step out of them to get down to only my white boxer briefs.

Laughing, Sara, comes up out of nowhere and throws a pitcher of water at me, soaking myself and the women hanging on me.

This causes the crowd of women to scream and go crazy, enjoying the very visible view of my cock through the white fabric, as I fuck the air fast and hard.

Sara lifts a brow and looks down at my dick bouncing. "You can thank my ass later, big guy."

Shaking my head, I wink at Sara, as money comes flying from all around me, women desperate to get as good a view as they can.

I notice two women come at me at the same time, before I hear yelling and see the taller of the two girls reach for the other one's hair, yanking her down to the ground.

Kage seems to be too preoccupied with trying to get laid, to notice, so I yank the taller girl away from the girl on the ground and throw her over my shoulder, stalking toward the door.

She immediately takes this as an invite to shove both her hands down the back of my wet briefs and squeeze my ass as I walk.

Lane grips my arm as I walk past him to get outside. "Another female behaving badly or is your ass trying to escape to go get laid?"

I bump him with my shoulder, too annoyed to answer his dumb ass question. I need to get this woman off me so I can get this night over with. "Move," I growl," as I walk past him and into the grass.

With quickness, I pull her off of me and set her back down to her feet. She just laughs and reaches for my dick as if I didn't just kick her out of the club.

She thinks this is all fun and games, but I don't take someone getting attacked around me as a fucking joke.

I yank her hands away from my dick and help her down to the ground so she won't fall over. "A cab will be called for you. Sit here and don't move."

Her eyes widen in disbelief when she realizes what just happened and that I'm about to leave her here. "Where are you going?" She yells at my back.

"Make sure she gets in a cab," I tell Lane as I walk past him and back into the loudness of the club.

Taking a second to breathe, I glance over at Kage to see him hold five fingers up. Five minutes. Five more fucking minutes and this night from stripper hell is over.

My ass is about ready to fall over from exhaustion, but these women need to leave here satisfied and ready to come back each week and it's my job to make sure that happens.

Nodding my head at Kage, I rush over to the other side of the room, where Kash is upside down on a chair, thrusting his hips in some girl's face.

Picking some random woman that catches my eye, I pull her chair away from the table and pick her up, so that her legs are wrapped around my waist.

I place her hands on my chest and run them down my body, while I move my hips against her to the music.

She covers her face with her free hand, embarrassed.

Not wanting to get mixed up in the crowd again for the night, I focus my attention on the brunette in my arms, until the last song finally ends.

I'm standing here completely drenched now, half-naked and sweating my ass off.

Kage, Kass and Lane must notice how much tonight has kicked our asses, because they make their way through the crowd and start clearing out the room, being sure to keep the women at a distance from us.

"Holy fuck!" Kash runs past me, naked, holding a wet shirt over his junk. "This is the busiest night we've ever fucking had here. I need a few shots after this."

"No shit," I bite out. "Three different bachelorette parties this weekend and they all decided to come on the same night."

Stone emerges from the crowd, with Sage wrapped around his waist. He's soaking wet like me and Kash, but Sage could care less.

She just grips onto his face, pulling him in for a kiss and letting every other girl in the room know that they can look, and maybe even touch, but she's the only one he's going home with.

They're closer than ever and I'm happy as hell for them.
After all they've been through, they deserve it.

Now to get the hell out of here before Kash tries dragging me out tonight . . .

AFTER THE LATE NIGHT I spent at *Walk Of Shame*, shaking my dick for money, all I really want is a moment of quiet and some time to pull my thoughts together.

To be away from the screeching sounds of women screaming and hands clinging to my every muscle, desperate to touch anything of me they can.

As fun as it is to have it so fucking easy, and know that I can have any girl that I desire, I want more than that. More than a quick fuck with a woman that simply wants me because I'm a popular male entertainer with a big cock.

I may give off the impression that I'm a man-whore that takes any hot woman to bed, but there's so much more to me than that. What I'm looking for can't be found inside the walls of a male strip club.

I'm a giver and when I find that right woman, I'm giving her everything that I fucking have in me. Seeing Stone and Sage together only makes me want that more.

Until then . . .

A knock sounds at the door of my office, and right away, I know who is on the other side.

It's a twenty-four-hour gym, but there's only one person that ever comes between the hours of two and three a.m.

Sophie Miller.

Standing up, I rub my hands down my face and walk over to unlock the door for her.

I may be tired and stressed as all hell, but having sex with

Sophie, distracts my mind for a few hours, at least twice a month.

She works late nights at another club and passes the gym on the way home, usually stopping if she sees my motorcycle parked outside.

Smiling, Sophie makes her way into my office, when I open the door for her. "Rough night?" She looks me over, her eyes filled with lust and need.

"Yeah," I breathe. "Fucking exhausted."

Dropping to her knees in front of me, she grips the button of my jeans and looks up at me with desperate blue eyes. "Hopefully not too exhausted. I need this."

Placing my bodyweight against the desk, I grab onto her red hair with both hands and close my eyes as she twirls her tongue around the head of my cock.

She takes me half way in her mouth a few times, before attempting to fully take me in, but ends up choking on my length.

As much as I'm enjoying her mouth on me, I don't have the patience or strength tonight to be here for hours.

"Stand up," I command. "Bend over my desk and hold on tight."

Without hesitation, Sophie stands up and bends over my desk, spreading her slender legs for me.

With force, I yank her jeans down, along with her panties, and slap her bare ass.

"You in a hurry tonight or something?" she questions, while squeezing the desk. "I didn't even get to finish."

"Yeah. It's been a long night. I was just about to leave before you showed up."

She reaches behind her and strokes my cock a few times. "Let's go then."

Pushing her head down on my desk, I pull out a condom

and slip it on, before slamming into her, letting my frustration out.

With each hard thrust, she grips onto the desk, knocking things over and reaching for anything close enough for her to grab.

"Oh shit, Styx! You seem a lot more stressed than usual."

"'Cause I am." Gripping her neck, I choke her from behind, taking her as deep as I can, not stopping until I feel myself ready to come.

Moaning, I pull out and release myself in the condom, taking a few deep breaths, before yanking the condom off, tossing it, and pulling my jeans back up.

Now I'm not one to go quickly and especially without getting my partner off first, but I just can't find it in me to give a shit tonight.

Sophie comes to stand in front of me, once she's redressed herself. "You really need to take a week off for a vacation or something and just focus on the gym and maybe . . . I don't know . . . fucking me more than just twice a month. I'm sure we both can relieve a lot of stress then."

Fighting to catch my breath, I kiss the top of her head, because I'm not a completely heartless ass. I may not want anything emotional with her, but she's not trash.

Just not the *one* for me.

"Yeah, I'll keep that in mind." I walk her to the door. "Be careful on your way home. It's late as shit and people are crazy. Call the gym if anyone messes with you."

She nods and smiles. "I always am. Got my mace handy at all times."

After letting Sophie out, I hang around the gym for about another hour, get a workout in and then head home for the night.

I'm off my shit tonight. Something just seems to be missing . . .

chapter TWO

Meadow

MY THIRD DAY WORKING A fourteen-hour shift at the hospital and I won't deny that I'm not completely exhausted both mentally and physically.

I love my job. I do, but sometimes it can just take so much out of you. You give so much and put your heart into everything that you do here, that you honestly don't have much of a life outside of taking care of patients and worrying about how they're doing when you're not around to take care of them.

I let out a small breath, and stand to my feet, when the call light from room 316 goes off for the third time in an hour.

"I've got it," I tell Mandy. "He's only going to ask for me anyway."

She lets out a tiny laugh and continues on with her business on the computer. "He always does. I don't even bother anymore when you're here."

"I don't blame you."

Walking into Henry's room, I stop next to his bed and place

my hand over his bruised one. "Anything I can help you with, Henry?"

He shakes his head and mutters at the TV mounted on the wall. "What is this garbage? It's been on all damn day."

I follow his eyes up to the TV and laugh. He always knows how to entertain the staff. "It wasn't on when I came in here about twenty minutes ago." Smiling, I hand the remote within his reach and point at the channel buttons. "You do know that this hospital has more than one channel right, Henry?"

He squeezes my hand and gives me a charming smile, although his dentures aren't in. "It makes an old guy happy when a pretty nurse is around to take care of him. It's about as much action as I can get these days."

"Oh I'm sure a guy like you can find a beautiful woman to take on a date. You'll be out in a few days, once your leg heals." I grab the remote from Henry and flip the channel to something that he might understand better and be more familiar with. "There you go. All set. Now I get off in twenty minutes, so Mandy and Kayla will be here to take care of you. Be nice to them. Don't let me hear that you're refusing your meds from them again."

He throws his arm up, waving me off. "They're not you."

Smiling, I pat his hand and start walking toward the door. "Yeah, well I can't be here twenty-four-seven. So behave yourself, old man."

"Yeah. Yeah."

Right as I'm walking out of Henry's room and closing the door just enough to give Henry some privacy, Jase winks at me and grabs my hand, pulling me around the corner and out of view.

Jase is probably about the most attractive male nurse that works here. As much as I try not to be physically attracted to one of my co-workers, you'd have to be blind not to notice him.

"Meet me in twenty by my car?" he whispers next to my ear. "I parked next to you again."

"Not tonight, Jase. I have a date with a new gym and I have *a lot* of stress to work off."

Jase looks around to make sure that no one is watching, before he slips his hand around my waist and pulls me closer to him. "I've been thinking about fucking you all day. It's been three weeks now. Take that crap out on me."

Lifting a brow, I place my hand on his firm chest and lightly push him away from me. "Yeah, well if I remember correctly, there's a few other nurses that have been keeping you quite busy. No thanks. I'm good."

Jase shakes his head and backs away from me, when Mandy walks over.

He tries to play it off as if he wasn't just trying to get into my pants, but the look Mandy gives me, tells me that she picked up on it.

"What did Henry want this time?" she asks with a grin.

"For me to change the channel for him." I give Jase one last look, before walking off with Mandy and listening to her tell a story about one of the other patients.

By the time I get done cleaning everything up and saying goodbye to my patients, I'm so tired that I consider just skipping the gym and checking it out another day.

But to be honest, I need to work off some stress and Jase won't be helping with that anymore.

BY THE TIME I MAKE it to the gym, and change into my gear, it's well past midnight. There's only a few other people in the gym, one of them on the treadmill next to me and the other two, lifting weights.

The two lifting weights keep looking my way, talking loudly about my *fine ass*, but I ignore them and try my best to not give them a piece of my mind. As if they can't make it any more obvious what they want to do to me. Not happening.

After thirty minutes on the treadmill, I look around me to see that the guys are still watching me, so I give up on the treadmill and decide to move somewhere more private where I can have a moment to let my emotions out.

There's no one back there to see just how much stress and pent up anger that I really have and if I stay here with these ogling jerkoffs then I'm going to end up taking my frustration out on them and not in a good way.

Slamming back some water, I take a few seconds to catch my breath, before shutting myself in the other room and grabbing the end of the battle ropes.

Gripping tightly onto the ropes, I start out with some power slams, before moving onto some outside circles. I move for as long as I can, until my muscles ache and lungs burn as I fight for air.

Then I toss the ends of the rope down and let out a small scream of anger and relief.

I don't even realize that I'm no longer alone, until I look up at the wall mirror and see a muscular guy with blonde hair and striking blue eyes.

His arms are crossed and he's leaning against the doorframe as if he's completely comfortable just watching me.

"How long have you been there?" I question out of breath.

He lifts a brow and steps into the room when I reach for my *Swig Savvy* water bottle, just to be reminded that it's empty.

"Here." He holds out a bottle of water. "Long enough to see that you must be thirsty from working all that frustration off."

Keeping my eyes on his, I grab the water, unscrew the cap and throw it back, almost emptying it.

His eyes slowly move from my eyes, down to my lips around the top of the bottle.

"You need me?" he questions.

I pull the bottle away and laugh, while still fighting to catch my breath. "For what?"

He moves closer to me and rubs his thumb over my mouth, wiping the excess water away. "To bring you a towel . . ." his eyes slowly scan me over, stopping on the sweat, dripping between my cleavage. "Or to help you work out some of that frustration?"

Keeping my eyes on his cocky, but surprisingly smooth ass, I tilt the water back until it's empty, then toss the bottle back to him.

"No, thank you." I flash him a sweet smile. "After this I plan to get wet anyway and work out my frustration on my own. I don't need any help with that."

Smirking, he lifts a brow in amusement. "I like a woman that can work out her own frustration once in a while. I'm not gonna lie . . ." Walking past me, he grips the battle ropes in his hands and squats. "It's really fucking hot."

Swallowing, I stand back and watch his muscles flex as he does some power slams, looking as if he has just as much or more stress than me to get out.

His tattooed arms and hands have me completely hypnotized and I have to admit that he's extremely hot in that bad boy kind of way.

He looks nothing like the uptight men I have dated in the past. None of them have been able to handle me, but I have a feeling that he'd be able to do that and more.

After a few minutes, he drops the ropes and turns to face me, his body dripping with sweat as he breathes heavily.

I find myself checking him out completely, my eyes moving lower to check out his thick legs and then back up to admire his firm chest that his shirt is now plastered to. "Thanks for the water. I suppose I owe you now."

I reach for my bag and pull out my spare water bottle and toss it to him. "Anything else I can get you?"

He grins. "You really want me to answer that?"

I take a step back as he takes a few steps toward me, practically backing me up against the wall.

Trying not to let myself enjoy his closeness too much, I place my hand on his sweaty chest and push back a bit. "I don't know yet," I say honestly. "I have a feeling that it might be something that I want, but don't need."

He moves his face around my neck, to whisper in my ear. "I second that . . . Meadow."

I give him a surprised look as he backs away and goes back to grab the ropes. "How do you know my name? Should I be running right about now?"

He winks. "Only if you want to."

With that, he starts on the ropes again, leaving me to either stand here and watch him like a creeper again, or leave.

I find myself smiling, slightly amused, as I let myself out of the room to find something else to keep me occupied.

I'm standing here, looking around to get familiar with the gym and how it's set up, when one of the guys that was watching me earlier, steps up beside me and grips my waist. "You look a little lost." He now squeezes my hip, letting out this creepy little moan as his eyes roam over my body. "Want me and my friend to show you around?"

Disgusted, I remove his hand from my hip, but he quickly replaces it as if he has the right to touch me if he wants.

"Get your fucking hand off of me before I break it off." I

push his hand from my body and walk away from him, hoping that he won't follow.

It does no good, because he ends up on the elliptical beside me, talking once again. "I love a girl with a little sass. My friend over here does too. It turns us on."

His friend appears next to me, watching me as he wipes his armpits off with a towel. "You single?"

"No," I bite out. "Now fuck off."

"Damn . . . those tits." I cringe as his eyes roam my body just as his friend's did. "And that-"

"She told you to fuck off," a voice booms, causing both the guys to look surprised and a little scared when the blue eyed cutie appears out of nowhere, looking extremely pissed off. "Get the fuck out, before I let you out myself."

The guy on the elliptical cusses under his breath and turns off the machine. "What's up, man. Didn't realize you were still here. We were just giving the lady a little company. No harm."

Not the least bit humored by the douchebag, he grabs both of the men's gym bags and walks to the door, opening it and tossing them both outside.

He holds the door open and turns back our way. "When a lady tells you to fuck off, you fuck off. Out. Now."

I raise a brow in humor and watch as the assholes argue with each other on the way out the door, not one of them brave enough to argue with the guy kicking them out of the gym.

He lets out a long breath and then walks past me and back into the room where he came from.

Jumping off the elliptical, I make my way over to the doorway and watch as he works the ropes again.

Watching him has me completely hypnotized again, until he turns around and notices me creeping on him.

A small smirk crosses his face, before he stops for a second to breathe. "Enjoying the view?"

I ignore his question and just smile, before walking away, grabbing my bag and making my way outside to see a motorcycle parked next to my truck.

When I go to open the door, I notice what looks like a flyer on my windshield. Grabbing it, I read it over, unable to hold back the smile that takes over, mixed with slight excitement.

"Holy. Shit."

Yup. Definitely different than the men I've dated and most likely a lot more trouble . . .

STYX

IT FEELS LIKE IT'S BEEN weeks since I've had a day off at the club, so I choose to enjoy it, by spending some time working on my motorcycle and throwing back a few beers.

I'm off in fucking La La Land, forgetting about everything else around me, until my father's shitty voice pulls me back to reality.

"Working on that old bike again. With all the money you make taking your clothes off, you think you'd purchase a new one and get rid of that junk."

Growling under my breath, I throw my torque wrench beside me and run my greasy hands over my face.

"What the fuck are you doing here?"

My father chuckles and walks further into my garage, getting comfortable, touching my damn things as if he owns the place. I don't even know what makes the piece of shit think that he's welcome in my home.

"Your mother wants you to come over for poker night.

Maybe you can bet some of that G-string money you bring in. Unless you're afraid to lose it to your old man."

Standing up, I kick my toolbox out of the way and reach for a towel to clean my hands. "You're not my fucking old man." I turn to face him so he can see all my hatred for him. "You're a piece of shit that beat me up almost every day of my childhood and ruined any hope I had growing up. And my mother . . . well she's stupid for taking you back and thinking that she can hide the bruises. I will always have her back and I'll always protect her, but I won't be accepting any invites to *her* home, anytime soon. Got it, *Old man?*"

He laughs. He actually fucking laughs.

The sound of his laughter snaps something in me, and before I know, I have him slammed against the wall with my hand wrapped around his throat.

I lean in close and give his throat a tight squeeze. "Let me see one more bruise on my mother and I will snap your neck without a second thought. Got it! I'm watching you. I'm always watching you. Don't forget."

My father's eyes widen for a split second, letting me see the fear in them, before he quickly masks it with his stupid laugh that I hate so much.

"You'll be the one breaking your mother's heart when I tell her that you won't be coming tonight?" He pushes me away from him and fixes his shirt. "Your mother thinks you hate her."

"Leave," I growl. "Before I throw you out myself."

He shrugs as if being thrown out is no big deal and walks until he's standing just outside the garage door. "You've always been full of excuses, son. So your mother should be used to the disappointment."

Rotating my shoulders in anger, I hit my fist against the garage door button, and watch the door close in front of the asshole that raised me.

He ruined my childhood and took everything away from me and my mother, yet she always takes his ass back as if there's nothing else out there for her.

That's exactly why I'll only settle down when I find *the* one. I don't plan to just give my heart to anyone and when I do find her, I'll give her everything of me.

Having *him* show up unannounced has me so screwed up in the head that the last thing I can concentrate on is working on my bike.

"Well fuck."

Going inside, I take a quick shower, before I hop on my bike and head back to my uncle's gym for the second time today.

Hell, I might as well call it mine, because he's planning on me taking over soon so he can focus on his family.

I've been here more in the last week than he has in the last six months.

James, one of the personal trainers, greets me when I walk in. "Hey, man. Back again?"

I open the door to my office and toss my bag inside. "Need to work off some more steam."

He looks me over with a small grin. "Fucking shit. You're the busiest person I know, man. Between working out all damn day and dancing at the club, I'm surprised that you even have time to breathe."

"Me too," I say as I walk past him and hit the weights.

After spending a few hours at the gym, I shower for the third time today, and head over to the club to have a few drinks.

Sara is working tonight, and she always finds a way to keep my mind busy and off all the bullshit.

"How's your dick?" she questions with a smirk. "Taking a break for the night?"

I raise a brow and tilt back my beer. "He's been getting more than a few breaks these days."

"I've noticed," she responds. "Good for you and your dick. I'm sure the fucker's tired."

"How about you? How's that girlfriend of yours?" I ask, making her turn red. "Never thought you'd give up the dick."

She slaps my forehead and leans in close to my face, talking against my lips. "Who says I've given it up? Having both is a lot more fun and I learn new tricks every day. You don't even know what I'm capable of these days, big guy."

I lift my beer to her and adjust my erection. "Might as well give me one more after that shit. Damn!"

She smirks and slides me another beer, jumping back in surprise as Kash jumps over the bar and reaches for the bar gun to spray his body down with water. "Ah yes. This feels so damn good."

"Stop moaning like that or I'll have to take you home to Kendal so we can take advantage of your sexy ass."

Kash raises a brow to Sara. "Damn . . ." he moans again, just to get a reaction of Sara. Then he looks over to see my un-amused face. "Lighten the hell up, man."

I close my eyes and growl when water hits my face and then my chest.

Both Sara and Kash laugh, before he throws the gun down and runs back over to the small crowd of women that are yelling for him.

Sara takes a few seconds to check me out now that my shirt is clinging to my chest, before speaking. "There's this sexy little blonde chick roaming around looking lost." She looks over my shoulder. "Looks like she's looking for someone and the boys don't seem to be it."

Setting my beer down, I turn around in my stool to see

Meadow, searching the room around her.

For some strange reason, my heart starts beating fast, wondering if she could be here for me. It's not even as if she would know to look for me here.

I hope like hell that she isn't here to see Kash or one of the security dicks.

"I'll be back." Standing up, I walk up behind her and listen to her talk to herself.

"What the hell am I doing here? This is ridiculous. I'm leaving." She turns around, running straight into my chest with a grunt.

"Looking for someone?" I question, while gripping her waist to hold her steady. "Leaving because you haven't found them?"

She smiles up at me and takes a step back. "Maybe." I follow her as she makes her way to the bar and orders a drink. After Sara brings her a beer and eye-fucks her, she turns back to face me. "So tell me again how you knew my name?"

I laugh as she eyes me over, her pale blue eyes spending an awful long time on my chest. "Is that why you're here? To find out if I'm a stalker or some shit?"

She walks away, leaving me no choice but to follow her again, as she takes a seat at a table, far away from the stage.

She lifts a brow when I sit down, as if that's her answer.

I look her up and down and pull her chair between my legs so that I can look her in the eye. "I should be asking you how you knew to find me here. Maybe *I* should be the one concerned for my safety."

Taking a swig of her beer, she gives me a look as if I'm crazy. "You left a flyer on my truck . . . *Styx*. I think you wanted me to find you."

Fucking Kash.

His ass thinks it's funny to come to the gym and leave flyers everywhere to make it aware to all of its members that I moonlight as a male entertainer.

There's been times that I've walked in to over a hundred flyers taped to the walls.

"So you came to see me strip?" I lock the leg of her chair in place with my leg and smile when she tries scooting back. "It's my night off, but I can give you a private dance if you want. I'll even do it for free since you look so fucking beautiful right now."

She about chokes on her beer, but clears her throat and plays it off, as if what I just said didn't excite her. "You always kidnap a girl's chair so she has no choice but to hang out with you?"

"No," I answer, honestly. "This will be the first. But I like you so . . ."

"So . . ." She laughs and pulls her pale hair into a bun, making me look at her arms and take notice of her sleeve of tattoos, covering her right arm. She was wearing a V-neck long sleeved shirt the other night, keeping her arms hidden. *Damn, that's sexy.* "You decide to stalk me and then keep me captive. Good game."

I wrap the single strand of hair, that hangs in front of her face, around my finger. "I know your name, because you work out at *my* gym. There was a new member signed up by the name, Meadow, and your gorgeous body was the only one that I didn't recognize."

We sit here and just stare at each other for what feels like five minutes, before Meadow stands up and pushes her chair in. "I should go. It's been a long night."

"Where?" I question.

"Where?" she questions back, confused as to what I'm asking. "Where what?"

"Where has it been a long night?"

"The hospital. Have a good night, Styx."

She walks away, leaving me to watch the sway of her perfect

ass, as she brushes right past Kash, not even stopping to take a second look.

In fact . . . I don't think she watched the guys dancing at all.

This has me jumping to my feet and rushing outside to catch her.

She lets out a sexy little laugh when she notices me following her. "What are you doing?"

"Walking you to your car."

She stops next to a huge truck and gives me the cutest fucking look. "Who says I drive a car? I like my rides big and fast."

Impressed, I watch her climb into her truck, before she reaches for the door. "Then you're going to love me." I smirk.

She tries to hide her smile, but completely fails as she pulls the door closed and drives away.

Holy fuck, this woman is different from the rest and I really badly want to find out in which ways . . .

chapter FOUR

Meadow

IT'S BEEN A FEW DAYS since I saw Styx at *Walk Of Shame* and for some reason . . . I can't shake him from my thoughts. I keep wondering about him and wanting to know more about this man.

He's a male stripper, everything that I should run away from, yet, I want to run back to the gym or club in hopes of seeing him again.

He intrigues me. Even though he comes on a little strong, I don't feel threatened by it. It doesn't make me feel creepy and dirty like those guys at the gym did.

Styx being up front with me, makes me like his company. It's usually exhausting trying to figure men out and what they're thinking. He comes right out and just says it. No holding back.

Jase watched me for weeks, confusing me and frustrating me, before he finally hit on me and told me what he wanted to do to me.

Just like my ex, Mack. The asshole that left me right after

my aunt died because he couldn't deal with my emotional state.

Although the strip club isn't my usual scene, I've talked Mandy into going with me tonight.

Yes, I want to see Styx with less clothing on . . . so sue me. I'm only human. The man is dangerously sexy.

"I can't believe I've let you talk me into this." Mandy shakes her head from beside me and jumps when a group of women scream in excitement when the DJ starts playing music. "Please tell me we don't have to stay here all night. My ears can't take it."

I laugh and hand her one of the Bomb Pop drinks that I ordered for us. "Just long enough to see Styx perform and then we can slip out and back to our cozy little lives."

"Let's hope he's up first then," she yells over the music, while fingering her dark hair. "This place is a little too wild for me."

We sit here for about ten minutes, before the first guy finally takes the stage. A gorgeous guy with tattoos and dark blonde hair humps his away across the stage, the women going crazy and screaming out the name *Kash*.

I recognize his picture from the flyer that was on my truck the other night.

He's been on stage for all of five minutes and already owns every single girl in this room. Not one person isn't watching this hottie get down and dirty.

Once it gets close to the end of the song, Kash, jumps down from the stage and dances against a few women, before bringing one up to the stage with him to dance above her face.

This is the first time that I've ever watched a male stripper, and I have to admit that it makes me feel sort of . . . hot.

Even though I was here a few days ago, my attention was on Styx and Styx alone. He's still the only reason I'm here now.

When I look over at Mandy, her face is red and her drink is

half gone already. "You going to survive over there?" I ask with a laugh. "Breathe."

She nods her head, keeping her eyes glued to the stage. "I had no idea that the strippers would be this hot. Most of the on-line videos have men with *amazing* bodies and not so great faces and I've seen *a lot* of videos."

I laugh at her confession. "Walk of Shame is the exception, I guess. There's got to be at least one decent male strip club out there and it looks like we're in it." I elbow her and smile, holding my straw to my lips. "Let's just enjoy the entertainment for a bit, even if Styx isn't up till last."

She nods her head in agreement. "This Kash guy is pretty damn entertaining. So I'm enjoying. You couldn't get me to leave now if you dragged me out that door by my hair."

Smiling, I sit back and enjoy the show, getting excited at the idea of seeing Styx dance. If he moves anything like this Kash guy, then I have a feeling that I'm going to like it . . . *a lot.*

I can't help but to hope that he spots me out in the crowd. For some reason, I want him to know that I'm here and to see his reaction to me showing up to watch him.

Another guy comes on next, instead of Styx, so I get up from my seat and walk over to order us a couple more drinks and two cherry bombs to waste some time.

A very tall, cute, security guard walks over and offers to carry my drinks for me when he notices me struggling.

"I got it, gorgeous." He grabs the drinks and smiles down at me. "Where you headed?"

"Over there." I point to where Mandy is practically standing to get a better view of the stage. "Thanks . . ." I stop and search for his name.

"Kage. And not a problem. Cale would kick my ass if I didn't offer to help a beautiful woman with her drinks."

He winks and then motions for me to walk first, then he sets the drinks down for us and smiles, before walking away.

"He's good looking too," Mandy points out. "This place is full of hot guys. Why have we not come here before?"

"Because the hospital is exhausting," I point out. "Plus, I'm not sure what the hospital would think of their nurses partying it up at the strip club, waving cash at half-naked men. Then showing up for our shift, hungover and still fantasizing about the eye candy we saw the night before."

She laughs. "That does sound bad. Maybe we should keep this private. I'm not even telling Kayla about this because she has a huge mouth."

"Oh, we're definitely keeping this between the two of us. Kayla is the last person who should find out. She'd run to that uptight bitch and have her on our asses, watching us even harder than she already does."

"Oh God. I'd have to find a new job then. Let's forget out the hospital and just enjoy before my excitement gets stomped out by thoughts of them."

We've been here for thirty minutes now and Stone is now leaving the stage.

Excitement courses through me at the idea that Styx could be next. I only saw three men on that flyer. Styx, Stone and Kash and we've already seen the other two.

The next song comes on so I sit up straight and grab my drink, prepared to see Styx comes out, looking sexy and tempting.

I'm a little disappointed when the other two guys walk out instead and start dancing on the main floor as if the individual shows are over for the night.

"Where's this Styx guy you were talking about? Is it his night off or something?"

I let out a breath of disappointment and grab my drink,

about ready to get up and drop it off at the bar to leave. "Maybe it is. Crap!"

Mandy's eyes shift to behind me and go wide when a pair of hands grip my waist. "Maybe not."

Quickly, I turn around to see Styx standing behind me, dressed in a pair of ripped up, faded jeans and a white tee, hugging his firm chest. "Couldn't get enough of me?"

A smile takes over as I watch him watching me. He looks extremely amused. "Thought I would catch a show and see what you're made of." I set my drink down and grab my purse. "Guess I picked a bad night."

He smirks and grips my hip when I try to walk away. "Or maybe you picked a good one."

Before I get a chance to respond, he grabs my hand and begins pulling me through the crowd. Girls grab at him from everywhere, screaming and going crazy, but he ignores them, stopping when we get to a hallway with private rooms.

"What about Mandy? I can't just leave her out there by herself."

"Kage is keeping her busy for the next twenty minutes." He lifts a brow and smiles. "You wanted to see what I'm made of, right? Now's your chance." He leans in close to my ear, his breath hitting my skin. "Unless you think you can't handle it. It's okay if you can't. A lot of women lose it behind these doors."

I nod my head in response, unable to form words that won't sound stupid at the moment.

Opening the door to the private room, he guides me inside and backs me up, until I'm sitting on a couch.

I swallow and begin shifting in my seat as Pony by *Ginuwine* comes through the speakers, causing Styx to grind his hips and run his hands down his chest and abs.

Between the darkness, the hot song, and his sexy dancing, I

instantly break out in a sweat, needing to fan myself off.

I can't believe that I'm watching the hot guy from the gym strip right now.

Moving to straddle my lap, he slowly grinds his hips against me, while running *my* hands down his body this time. Every dip of muscle feels so damn good beneath my fingers, that I find myself getting wet, just thinking about them flexing above me.

"What?" he questions with a cocky smile. "Like the way my body feels under your hands?"

Biting my bottom lip, I grab his nipple through the fabric and twist the bar a little. "I'd be lying if I said I didn't," I admit.

He leans in close to my ear and presses his lips against me. "Don't be afraid to touch me *anywhere* you want. This is your moment to live out any hot little fantasy that's running through your head right now with no judgement." He thrusts his hips against me and grips my hair so damn sexy that my pussy clenches. "It's just the two of us."

Pulling away from me, he sits up straight and yanks his shirt off over his head.

My eyes widen when I take in just how glorious and beautiful his body truly is. Every tattooed muscle has me wanting to trace the outline for hours.

I'd use my tongue on Styx.

He surprises me by picking me up and wrapping my legs around his waist.

Looking me in the eye, he backs me up, pressing me against the wall. Then he pins my hands above my head, thrusting me up with his hips as if he's fucking me.

I let out a little moan, lost in the moment, as he rotates his hips and slows down, looking me right in the eye. His eyes stay locked on mine as if he's daring me to look away, but I don't. I can't.

He's hard now and I can feel his thickness pushing against me.

It's so extremely hot that I can just feel myself getting wetter with each move of his hips and completely turned on by this man.

Something about the way he's dancing for me just seems so intimate and deep.

I lean my head back and close my eyes, when I feel his lips press against my neck and his hands cup my face.

It feels good so I allow it to happen for a few moments, until I feel his lips press down next to mine.

"No," I whisper, as I turn my face. "I don't know you, Styx."

He seems to like this response, because he smiles as if I've just proved something to him. "Good."

Backing me away from the wall, he places me back on the couch and steps away to strip out of his jeans.

My heart jumps out of my chest with excitement when I look down at his tight boxer briefs to see just how hard and huge that he really is.

Stepping up on the couch, he grabs my hands and places them on his abs. He looks down at me, his ice blue eyes burning into me. "The song's almost over."

I know exactly what that means.

My heart races even faster, trying to decide if it's right to do what I really want to do with his body.

No judgement.

With my heart racing, I slowly lower my hands and brush them over his large erection, being careful not to spend too much time on his dick, before gripping his thighs.

The last thing I want to do is violate him and be one of those screaming women in the next room.

He smiles down at me and climbs down from the couch,

when the song ends.

"Did you feel what you expected when first coming to my room?"

I shake my head. "No. I felt so much more."

Standing up, I allow myself to check him out one more time in this no judgement room. "I wasn't expecting it to feel so . . . I don't know. It was good."

He laughs. "You wanted to see what I was made of . . ." he reaches for his jeans and slips them back on, leaving them undone. "That wasn't all of me, yet."

We both just stare at each other, until the door opens and what appears to be another security guard, pops his head inside. "Cale's looking for you. He's about to leave so you might want to hurry."

He gives him a nod, while keeping his eyes on me. "Tell him I'll find him in a minute, Kass."

"Sure thing, man."

Styx finally pulls his eyes away from me and runs his hands over his sweaty face. "I'll see you around?"

I smile. "Maybe."

He grabs his shirt and laughs, while backing up out the door.

I release a deep breath and smile while fighting for breath.

Seriously?

Styx is insane when it comes to dancing to turn women on. He was definitely no disappointment.

Feeling the need to get out of this place so I can breathe again, I rush out of the private room, fighting my way through the crowd to get to Mandy.

I'm dragging her out of here, even *if* it has to be by her hair.

Seeing Kash straddling her lap, I cuss to myself, knowing that I'm about to ruin her fun if I drag her out.

I stand back for a few minutes and watch him grind against

her instead.

Holy hell, this man does it extremely well too. I'm getting hot again, just picturing Styx back in my lap, grinding me like that.

As soon as Kash stands up and she shoves money into the side of his briefs, I yank her from the chair and drag her with me through the room, until we're finally back outside where I can catch my breath.

Holy shit . . . Styx's dance was the hottest moment of my life and the wet dream that I'll be having for the next week . . .

STYX

CALE PULLED ME ASIDE THE other night to offer me a couple days off from the club. He must've been able to tell how stressed I've been for the last week since business has exploded.

I told him that I didn't need time, but he kept pushing, telling me that the last thing he wants is to stress his guys out. He said if it came down to it that he could ask Hemy to take on a couple days to cover me.

So I agreed to the next two days off.

Pulling my motorcycle up to the second hospital that I've been to today, I kill the engine and set my helmet on the seat.

I tried just sitting at home and relaxing for once, but it didn't work out so well. Apparently, I have to always be doing something or else my mind goes places that it doesn't need to be. Relaxing is out of the fucking question for me.

Walking into the building, I step up to the information desk and smile at the lady when she looks up. "I'm looking for Meadow . . ."

She immediately points down the hall, toward the elevator, enthusiastically. "Ms. Jenkins is on the third floor. Just go down to the elevators and then take a right once you get to the third floor."

I flash her a grateful smile, which causes her to blush and smooth out her blouse. "Thank you, Anne."

"Anytime." She smiles back and then watches me all the way down to the elevators.

Once I get to the third floor, a couple of young nurses walk by, checking me out and whispering not so softly, about the things they'd do to me.

But the only thing I'm focused on is finding Meadow and seeing how she reacts to my ass just showing up at her work out of the blue.

She surprised the hell out of me and I figured I need to return the favor.

I walk down the long hall, peeking into the opened door rooms, until I spot Meadow changing the sheets on one of the beds, while chatting with her friend that was at the club with her last night.

Smiling, I stand back and watch her work. It's only fair after she did the same to me.

" . . . I'm not doing anything tonight. Going home. And going to bed. I told you."

"You're trying to tell me that you're not going back to the club tonight to look for Styx? You want to see him again. I can tell." Her friend laughs. "You've had this look on your face all day . . ."

Meadow's head shoots up to look at her friend. "What kind of look is that?"

"A one of longing . . . and horniness."

Turning red, Meadow grabs for a pillow and tosses it at her

friend's head. "Oh shut it! You don't know what you're talking about. I'm not . . . you're insane."

"Is she?"

Both girls look over at the sound of my deep voice.

Meadow tries hard to hide her smile, but there's no mistaking the fact that she's happy to see me here.

"Yes," she says, while pushing her friend away. "Mandy is extremely insane. So just ignore the words that come out of her mouth."

I raise a brow and look her over in her uniform, looking so damn cute. I can think of many ways that I'd like to strip her from it.

"Maybe I like the words that are coming out of her mouth. Especially the ones about you."

Mandy clears her throat and begins backing toward the door. "I'll be at the desk if you need me." She turns to me and smiles. "I'm not insane. Trust me, I know how to read my friend."

"Mandy!" Meadow looks at Mandy with wide eyes and points at the door. "Go!"

I wait for her friend to leave, before I walk into the room and greet her with a kiss on the cheek. "It's good to see you." I grab the back of her neck and look her in the eyes. "I'm not going to lie . . . I like what your friend was saying."

She lets out a small breath and turns her head away to hide her blush. "I'm surprised to see you here." She continues on with fixing the bed. "Was I easy to find? Or did you use some special stalker skills?"

My eyes lower down to her perfect ass when she bends over to tuck the sheet in. I'm trying really damn hard not to just walk up behind her and show her just how much she turns me on. "Doesn't matter. I had all day to search and I was on a mission."

This causes her to laugh and look up from the bed. "That

bored, huh?"

She stands up straight to walk around me, but I block her with my body and slide both of my hands under her neck to look her in the eyes. She holds my stare and her breathing picks up as I lean in close to her mouth. "Spending time with you happens to excite me, Meadow. That doesn't happen very often. Not many women can stay on my mind for longer than twenty minutes. You've been on mine for days."

I pull away and watch her throat as she swallows. "What are you doing in a few hours?" she questions. "Do you have plans?"

Reaching out, I wrap a strand of her hair around my finger and then push it behind her ear, brushing my thumb over her cheek. "Picking you up from work and taking you on a ride. I want to get you alone."

"Meadow," a male voice calls out from the doorway. "Everything okay in there?" He's trying to sound concerned, but jealousy is evident in his tone.

She sucks in a surprised breath, as I wrap my arm around her waist and pull her against me. I'm not worried about what he thinks, but it somehow feels like she might be.

That tells me that she's either talking to this guy or has in the past.

"I'm fine, Jase. You can go."

I look up from Meadow, when his footsteps enter the room. "She said you can go, Jase. She's perfectly fine in my hands. She hasn't complained yet."

This pretty boy is the complete opposite of me: dark hair, dark eyes, no facial hair or tattoos from what I can see at least.

He might've been able to show her a good time in the past, but that was before I came along.

He flexes his jaw as he looks us over, looking heated. My arm is still around her waist, and she hasn't made a move to change that. "I'll be right outside if you need me."

Meadow nods and lets out a frustrated breath. "I said . . . I'm fine. You can go."

Jase sizes me up one more time, before he finally turns for the door and disappears.

"Sorry about that. He's just . . ."

"Someone that wants you as badly as I do." I release my hold on her and walk toward the door. I stop and look back at her, once I reach the door. "Looks like I'll need to step my game up. See you soon, babe." I wink and then walk off, looking Jase over as I pass him in the hall.

He might think he has a chance at this point, but when I want something, I give it my all. And right now, I'm thinking what I want is Meadow.

Eyes focus on me again as I make my way toward the elevator, the same nurses as before, watching me and trying to decide who should come talk to me.

That gets broken up when Jase walks past and tells them to get busy. One of the nurses gives him a dirty look, but they all scatter anyway and go their separate ways.

The elevator opens and I'm not surprised when Jase steps in after me.

Smiling to myself, I press the button to the lobby and wait for him to speak, because I know he has something to say. He's threatened by me.

The ride down is silent. I keep my eyes on him, letting him know that I'm waiting for him to tell me what's on his mind.

It's not until the elevator doors open that he finally speaks. "Stay away from Meadow. She's mine."

Smiling, I step out of the elevator and catch the door right as it's about to close. He looks up at me, surprised. "She won't be for long."

I turn and walk away, knowing that this asshole is full of shit.

I'm not going anywhere until Meadow tells me to and the look in her eyes whenever I'm around, tells me that it won't be anytime fucking soon . . .

chapter SIX

STYX

THE PERSON IN FRONT OF me is driving like an asshole, slamming on their brakes every few minutes. All it's doing is pissing me off and testing my patience.

"What the fuck!" I yell out in frustration when they do it again, almost causing me to slam into them.

I'm so close to jumping off my motorcycle at the next stoplight and teaching this fucker how to drive.

They're riding the ass of the Honda in front of them and that's when I notice that the Honda is brake checking the idiot in front of me.

Frustrated as all hell, I go to switch lanes, just to have the asshole in front of me decide at the last second that they want to get over, without looking first.

The car swipes the front tire of my motorcycle, making me lose control. My helmet takes a hard hit, bouncing off the street, before I slide across the road with my motorcycle half way on top of me.

"Fuck!" I scream out in pain once I come to a stop, and punch the road, pissed off that the asshole in front of me just hit me.

My motorcycle is further down the side of the road all banged up, causing other cars to slam on their brakes and stop to check on me.

I feel the pain radiate up into my shinbone, when I roll over and attempt to stand to my feet. I most likely have a broken ankle. I've felt this pain before. More times than I'd like to admit. I have my father to thank for that.

Fuck! I take my helmet off and slam it down, fighting to control my anger.

"Don't move!" An older guy yells when he reaches me. "You hit your head pretty hard. I called 9-1-1. Stay still, you might've hurt your back or neck."

One of the other drivers that saw what happened is arguing with the asshole that hit me and I want nothing more than to hobble other there my damn self and give him a piece of my mind, but there's two people fighting to keep me still now.

Thankful for the husband and wife who cared enough to stop and help me, I don't fight them to move. I just lay here and wait for the ambulance to arrive, telling myself that I'll find that fucker and kick his ass later.

After I get asked a few questions and hoisted into the back of the ambulance, I give them orders to take me back to Meadow's hospital. They want to take me somewhere else, but I tell them to fuck off and take me where I want them to.

I know if I complain enough that they'll do it and they do.

Once I get to the emergency room, and give them a short medical history and answer some more questions, I get an X-ray that comes back as a small break to my ankle and am told that I'm stuck in this fucking walking boot for up to six weeks. I hope like hell it's a lot less time than that or else I'll be spending my time dancing in a damn chair.

I'm given some medication for the pain after a while and then moved up to the third floor, to make space in the emergency room.

Since I hit my head pretty good, they want to keep me over night so that someone can be around to wake me up every few hours.

I keep looking for Meadow as they roll me down the hall and into my room and it isn't until right after I get into my room, that I see Meadow walk past, stopping as soon as her eyes land on me.

For as long as I've been here, it has to be about time for her shift to end by now.

I can hear her outside talking to another nurse, but can't make out what they're saying. All I know is that she sounds concerned and keeps telling the other nurse that she's fine.

Closing my eyes, I let out a small breath and run my hands through my hair, frustrated by this whole situation.

I should've been picking Meadow up on my motorcycle right about now and getting her the hell away from everyone so we could be alone.

Instead, I'm stuck here in this stupid bed and she's about to leave for the night.

A few minutes later, Meadow enters the room and places her hand on my head, softly caressing it. "Damn, Styx. What the hell happened? Are you alright? Does your ankle hurt bad?"

I smile up at her because all I can think about is pulling her into this bed with me and pleasuring her to help pass the time and make this stay enjoyable. I'm sure my lips on hers could ease a lot of this pain I'm feeling right now.

"Some asshole hit me. I still have use of my important body

parts, so I'm good. Want to join me?" I pat the bed beside me.

She smiles, her cheeks slightly pink and starts messing around with the monitor, checking things. "I bet you are. I have a feeling that it takes a lot to keep a guy like you down."

"So . . . is that a no?" I question, jokingly just to see her smile again.

"If I said yes, I'd lose my job." She turns to face me and looks me over in my gown. "I have a feeling things wouldn't be so quiet next to you. Especially when you have easy access to your dick and you look so cute in that gown." She winks and adds, "I'll be sure to keep the other nurses away."

Once I look up and realize what time it is, I raise my brows in question and watch her working as if she's in no hurry to get out of here. "Didn't your shift end ten minutes ago?"

"I decided to work a double so I can keep an eye on you and make sure that you get woken up. We're short staffed and if I leave then you won't get the attention you need and I want to make sure that you're well cared for."

Well, fuck. She's staying for me. Is it wrong that that makes me so fucking hard?

"And you want to give me that attention?" I tease. "Looks like that ride will have to wait a bit unless you want an audience."

"You're a jokester, aren't you? A jokester and a stalker who likes to capture girl's chairs to make them stay and talk to them. Good combination." She smiles and leans down close to my face. "Get some rest. I'll be close by."

I smile and attempt to get as comfortable as I can in this shitty bed. I still wish I could get her to join me. Knowing that she'll be close by will only make me want it more. "That will keep me up all night."

"I'll be back. Just get some rest before I break your other ankle. Got it."

I close my eyes and grin as she walks away, leaving me alone to think of all the ways I can keep her as my own.

Damn this woman has just given me another reason to make me want her even more now . . .

I WAKE UP IN THE middle of the night to Meadow rubbing my head and bringing me some fresh water for when I wake up thirsty.

I feel her lift the blanket to check the swelling on my ankle, but I'm exhausted so I keep my eyes closed and just enjoy having the presence of someone in the room that cares.

She already woke me up an hour ago, so there's no real need for her to be in here right now. Not yet.

The guys said they'd stop by to see me, but I told them no, that I'd rather them just get some sleep and visit me when they get off work tomorrow night.

I didn't need them feeling like they *had* to waste time watching me lay in this stupid bed over a busted ankle.

Meadow thinks that I'm sleeping, but I peek over her way and watch as she takes a seat in the chair and closes her eyes.

She's exhausted and I can see it taking over her as she rubs her face and yawns repeatedly. Makes me feel guilty that she stayed to keep her eye on me.

"I'm fine," I say tiredly. "You should go home and get some sleep."

She opens her eyes and stands up. "Drink up."

I reach for the glass and slam back the water. "My head and ankle are fine and I'll be out of here in a few hours. You should go."

"Yeah, I was thinking about taking off. Jessie will be the nurse to get you out of here in the morning. I just wanted to say bye before I left, but didn't want to wake you again so soon. How are you feeling? In any pain?"

She doesn't look too happy at the idea of this other nurse caring for me, but she's already barely able to stay awake. Maybe she likes me more than she's ready to admit.

I'll just have to change that.

"It doesn't hurt much. It's nothing I haven't dealt with before."

"Ok good." She looks a little disappointed as she steps closer to me.

"I'll be back to take you on that ride. Don't worry," I tease. "I keep my word."

She laughs and adjusts my pillow, getting so close that her lips almost touch mine. I'm half tempted to close the distance between us, but I want to wait until she's awake enough to enjoy the feel of my lips capturing hers. "Maybe you will. Maybe you won't. Goodbye, Styx. Get some sleep."

All I can do is smile and watch as she walks away. This woman just sacrificed her whole night and sleep to be here for me.

That's something I'll never fucking forget and I'm more thankful than she knows. I'll make it up to her.

I lay here for a good twenty minutes or so, before I finally start falling back to sleep.

Of course, I fall sleep, while planning my return to take her on that motorcycle ride that I promised.

She may think that I'm not coming back for her, but I am. That's a promise . . .

chapter SEVEN

STYX

I'VE SPENT THE LAST TWELVE days bartending, while sitting on this damn stool, waiting on my ankle to heal.

I don't mind bartending once in a while, but it's far from being easy when you have to get up and hobble around for the right bottle of liquor every five seconds.

The women seem to think it's sexy as hell and have been giving me almost more attention than I do when I'm out on the floor dancing.

Almost every drink that gets ordered comes with an offer to take me home and fuck me until my ankle doesn't hurt anymore.

It's like they like the idea of taking advantage of me and want to keep me for as long as they can.

A little too late for that shit. I've turned every offer down. The only woman I've been thinking about taking me to bed is Meadow.

She's been all I can think about since she left me in that hospital bed and I don't think I'll be able to keep my hands off her the next time I get the chance to touch her.

I just want to make it through the next couple of weeks and get this ankle healed so that I can ride my motorcycle again. I promised Meadow I'd be back for her and I still plan on it.

Cale offered me a few weeks off work to heal, but since Hemy is still a part time bartender and will be dancing to cover me, I told Cale that I'd cover for Hemy behind the bar.

Plus, sitting at home does nothing good for my head. Too much shit runs through it and going to the gym just to sit behind my desk is boring as shit. The club is the only option for me at the moment.

"Are you sure I can't take you home and get you comfortable in my bed?" The beautiful woman in front of me points to her equally attractive friend. "We can both take your pain away. We promise it will be worth it."

Sara rushes over and leans over the counter, annoyed with everyone taking so much time to order drinks from me. "Order your damn drinks. There's a line behind you. You're not getting Styx's dick so move on."

I lift my brows as Sara walks away to help her side of the bar. Damn, I love that woman sometimes.

"You heard the boss. Now, what can I get you besides my cock, ladies?"

One of the girls starts rambling on about some kind of special drink that she wants, but all I can focus on is what looks like the back of Meadow's head, walking away.

I hop off the stool on my good leg, bouncing around to try to get a better view to see if it's really her, but there's too many heads in my way to get a good look.

It's not until she's walking out the door, that I get a view of the side of her face as she says something to Lane, before disappearing outside.

"Fuck. I'll be back," I tell Sara.

"Dammit," she says to my back as my crippled ass hops over the bar and almost falls over the other side. "Don't hurt your damn-self. Geez, Styx."

I ignore her and fight my way through the crowd, getting felt up by pretty much everyone in my path.

By the time I reach the door and break free of the crowd, I get outside and look around, but don't see Meadow's truck anywhere.

Disappointment sets in as I run my hands through my hair in frustration.

I've been wanting to stop by the hospital and thank her, but I promised I'd be back on my motorcycle to take her on that ride.

I still have at least three weeks of healing before I can make that happen and I'm making every second of it worth the wait for her.

I just hope she'll still be excited to see me by then . . .

chapter EIGHT

Meadow

THREE WEEKS LATER...

I CAN'T CONTAIN MY EXCITEMENT when I get off work to see Styx leaning against his motorcycle, waiting for me in the parking lot.

My reaction only confirms how much I've actually been looking forward to seeing him again. I've been at the gym a few times since his accident, but didn't expect him to be there since my shift has been so messed up lately. I even stopped at the bar one night, but saw him surrounded by women at the bar, so I left, knowing that I'd never get the chance to talk to him.

Now, he's here and I feel this rush that I can't contain. My heart is going crazy as I look him over.

He's dressed in a leatherjacket, old faded jeans and a pair of biker boots. He looks so sexy and badass, like he's straight from a damn movie that all of us women fantasize about.

Forget the motorcycle . . . I want to ride him.

"You ready? Told you I'd be back to take you for a ride." He grabs my bag and tosses it in my truck, before grabbing my hand and helping me onto the back of his bike.

My heart does a little jump, when he reaches for my arms and wraps them around his muscular body. He feels so damn good. "Hold on to me and don't let go. I tend to like to ride fast and hard."

"Your ankle?" I question in surprise at the fact that he's already back on his motorcycle. It hasn't even been six weeks yet.

"The pain is gone and I've been walking on it for days now. I'm good as new. Now hold on tight."

"Where are we going?" I question as he slides his helmet on my head.

"Somewhere I like to go to clear my head."

He takes off and I hold on as tightly as I can, leaning my face into his strong back. The scent of his cologne is one of the sexiest things I've ever smelled and it does nothing to make me want him less right now.

As if him showing up for me, looking as incredible as he does wasn't enough.

We ride for a while, just enjoying the night air, before he turns down a trail, hidden by trees. Something about him taking me to the middle of nowhere has my body buzzing with excitement and wonder.

I'm not used to men wanting to go anywhere other than the bedroom or a bar.

It's nice because I like places where I can relax and clear my head away from everyone.

Once we reach the end of the trail, he parks next to water that I didn't even know existed, hidden back here.

We sit here for a few moments, before he helps me off his bike and hops off himself, taking off his jacket and draping it over my shoulders.

"Thank you," he whispers across my lips.

"For what?" My eyes lower to his lips, before slowly moving back up to meet his eyes. "I was just doing my job."

He licks his lips and fingers a strand of my hair. "You didn't have to stay and we both knew it. You stayed because you wanted to take care of me."

I swallow and take a step back from him. The way his eyes look into me as if he can see into my soul makes me feel as if I'm coming undone for him. He's so good at making me turn away first. "You're welcome," is all I can say.

He looks me over in silence for a few seconds as if he's trying to read me, before speaking again.

"I love how quiet it is back here. No screaming, whistling or a room full of women calling out my name and telling me all the things they want and expect me to do to them. This place brings me peace . . . a place where I can think about what I want in life."

He grabs my hand and pulls me down closer to the water, helping me up onto a huge rock to sit. Then he climbs up himself and pulls me to sit between his legs.

"What do you want in life?" I question, quietly, as he pulls my hair back and presses his lips against my neck.

It feels so good, making me forget my own worries and stress for just a short moment.

"I want a woman to love and build a life with. I want someone to take care of and cater to. I want to prove to myself that I'm not my asshole father and I have more to give than he ever did or has. I want to be a good man that is worthy of love."

His confession has me turning in his arms and cupping his face in my hands. I knew there was something deeper to him than meets the eye. "We all have a choice to be different than our parents and choose our own path." I pause and swallow back the emotions that are coming up. "I lost my parents when I was just ten and then my aunt last year so I've had no other choice than to be myself and go my own path. I barely even remember how my parents were."

"I'm sorry," he says gently.

I smile at the genuine look on his face. There's something about the way he looks right now that is extremely beautiful and real. "It's okay. I've been pretty good at being strong and I don't plan to stop anytime soon."

"I can see that and feel that about you and I like it. A strong woman is what I need and want in my life."

I feel myself blush and suddenly, I'm feeling playful, remembering our little joke from when we first met. "Is that why you continue to stalk me? Can't get enough of me, huh?"

His eyes lock with mine, before he grabs my face and runs his thumbs over my lips. "You're so fucking beautiful right now. I know you don't know me, but I have a feeling that I want you to."

Leaning in, he pulls my bottom lip into his mouth, before releasing it and breathing against my lips. "I may be acting tame as fuck around you, but truthfully, being around you makes me feel wild as hell and all I can think about is tasting every inch of you." He runs his tongue over his bottom lip. "Don't let my need to respect you make you believe that I don't want to fuck you so hard that you'll feel me for weeks. If you were any other girl, you would've been naked in the first ten minutes. That's the truth."

"Stop talking," I demand.

He's making me fucking wild inside. Something inside tells me that I should run, while the other part wants to jump on him and take him for a ride.

Jumping down from the rock, I take a few steps back, watching him as he watches me with those damn eyes that I can't get enough of.

He looks so calm and cool, watching me with a confidence that is extremely sexy to me. Even though his words shouldn't work on me, and turn me on, they have . . . completely.

Standing up, he silently jumps down from the rock and walks toward me, stripping his jacket from my shoulders and watching me breathe as the jacket hits the ground.

Before I can even consider what he's about to do, his lips are on mine and my legs are wrapped around his strong waist, his hands firmly gripping my ass.

His lips capture mine, completely, his lips owning me and making me forget everything around me. I don't even notice that we're walking toward the water, until we're waist deep and the cold water is creeping up my stomach, chilling me.

I grip onto him and raise my body higher to escape the water. "Why are we in the water? It's freezing!"

He presses his body into me, making it aware that he's completely hard. "Trying to make this erection go down, before I give in and fuck you like I want to."

"Oh . . ." I swallow and then let out a moan as he presses his erection into me again. "God, that feels so good. Don't do that. Please . . ."

He smiles against my lips and grinds his hips into me again, making me moan from the sensitivity. "Just because I'm trying to hold back from fucking you, doesn't mean I don't want to make you come."

Wrapping his hand in my hair, he tugs and digs his hips into me, while walking us over to the ground and laying me down, so that we're out of the water.

A small breath escapes me as he positions himself between my legs and reaches between our bodies to undo my jeans.

"Styx," I breathe.

"Don't worry," he says thickly. "I already said I'm not going to fuck you."

I lean my head into the ground as he slips his fingers into my underwear and runs his fingers through my slickness, making me even wetter.

"Fuck me . . . Meadow. You're so fucking wet for me."

I moan and nod my head as he slips a finger inside and slowly begins pumping in and out.

"Oh my god . . ." I moan and thrust my hips as he picks up speed and leans in to run the tip of his tongue over my lips.

The way he's working my pussy is more like a massage and he knows exactly what he needs to do to get me off.

He's not moving too fast and rough like most guys that selfishly try to get you off so they can just get the job done. No . . . he's working my pussy and owning it as if it's his only care and he's not stopping until my body is in full ecstasy.

Listening to his heavy breathing above me as he gets me off, has me craving to return the favor. So I rub his cock through his jeans, making him growl out and reach to undo his button with his free hand.

He moves his jeans and briefs down his waist, giving me just enough room to pull his erection out.

It feels so full and heavy in my hand, my fingers unable to reach fully around it as I stroke his length.

"Shit . . ." he moans. "This was supposed to be about getting you off. I was trying not to be selfish with you."

I wrap my arm around his neck and pull him down to press my lips against his. He moans into my mouth as I squeeze his cock, holding on for dear life as I come undone with his fingers inside me.

My moans escape once he releases my mouth.

"Oh . . . fuck . . . holy shit!"

Smiling down at me, he slips his fingers out and sucks them into his mouth. "You taste as sweet as you fucking look."

Every word that leaves his mouth only has my body craving for him even more, wanting to do very dirty things with him.

He roughly bites my bottom lip, before releasing it and kissing my neck. "Let's get you in my jacket and in my arms. It's cold."

I shake my head and grab his hips as he stands up and reaches his hand out. I shake my head, refusing it. "You haven't gotten off yet."

Looking down at me, he wraps both hands into the back of my hair and watches me as I slowly swirl my tongue around the head of his dick.

I do this a few more times, causing him to moan out and pull at my hair. "I need you to stop," he growls out, while stopping me from taking him in my mouth. "Stop, Meadow."

Confused, I look up at him as he grabs my hands to help me up. "What's wrong?"

Pulling me against him, he gently yanks my head to the side and presses his lips below my ear. "Because your mouth on me is making it fucking impossible to not rip that sexy little thong off and bury myself deep inside your tight little pussy. I only have so much restraint."

I watch him as he pulls his jeans back up and buttons them. "Should we go?" I ask as I fix myself.

He shakes his head and picks his jacket back up, draping it over my shoulders to warm me. "Not yet. Come on."

We end up back on the rock in the same position as we were before.

His arms wrapped around me.

Me between his thick thighs.

No words are exchanged.

We just sit here.

Both lost in thought.

Everything else in the world forgotten for the moment as we sit here with wet clothes and shoes, staring up at the sky.

Just two broken people enjoying each other's comfort for a short time.

I have a feeling I can get used to this . . .

STYX

SHE'S FALLEN ALSEEP IN MY arms, but I refuse to move and wake her up. I haven't moved a muscle in over twenty minutes now, not wanting to disturb her peace.

A hard working woman deserves every moment of sleep and comfort she can manage to get and I'll give her every second of it tonight.

Once she's ready to go, then I'll get my sleep. But until then . . .

I close my eyes and breathe in the peacefulness of the night air. Being here with Meadow in my arms will probably become one of my favorite memories of this place.

I've had lots of memories here, but all alone. There hasn't been one woman before Meadow, that I've wanted to bring out here and enjoy this spot with.

My arms loosen around her, when she stirs in my arms and whispers something.

I stay quiet, unsure if she's just talking in her sleep or if she's just woken up.

"Crap, I'm sorry," she speaks up louder this time, before

turning in my arms. "I'm more tired than I thought, I guess."

"No worries." I hop off the rock and pick her up, helping her down to her feet. "Let me get you home."

I grab her hand and guide her back to my motorcycle, before slipping my helmet back on her head and hopping on.

She holds on tightly, resting her head against my back the whole ride back to the hospital.

Once I pull up behind her truck, I help her off my motorcycle and grab her hand as she's about to walk away.

She gets ready to say goodnight, but I cut her off by pressing my lips against her, causing her to moan into my mouth and reach out to grip my hair.

"Holy shit," she whispers when I pull away. "Goodnight, Styx."

"I'll follow you home to make sure you get there safely. It's late."

She shakes her head and slides my helmet over my head with a cute little smile that makes me want to bite her lips. "I'll be fine. I'm house sitting for Mandy and she only lives like three minutes from here."

"I'll follow anyway," I argue. "I don't give up so easily so don't try."

"Alright. Well thank you." She backs away, keeping her eyes on me, until she's hopping into her truck.

This woman has a lot to learn about me if she thinks I won't protect her any chance that I get . . .

STYX

I'M STILL SURPRISED AS HELL with the restraint I showed with Meadow last week. It took everything in me to make myself stop her from sucking my cock and to not fuck her on the spot.

With any other woman, I would've had her screaming my name within the first ten minutes of being alone.

There's just something about Meadow that makes me want to be different with her. I've never had this feeling before, so I'm going to do everything I can to not fuck it up for as long as I can.

Now that I'm back to my long nights at the club, I haven't run into Meadow at the gym. We always seem to miss each other, and no matter how hard I've tried to get here so that I don't miss her, there's always someone at the club on my nuts, trying to hold me up.

Last night, I missed Meadow by five minutes. Five fucking minutes and it pisses me off.

I've been checking her log for the last week and she always

seems to show up around twelve-thirty and leaves just before two.

Last week had been a late week for all of us at the club, but I'm making sure that I get my ass out of there early tonight. I don't care what it takes.

Logging onto the gym's membership info, I look up Meadow's information for what seems like the hundredth time in the last five days since I've seen her.

Her phone number is staring back at me, tempting me to add it to my phone so that I can reach her whenever I want.

I don't usually do this with women or members of the gym, due to their privacy, but the more I look at her number, the more I decide to say fuck the rules.

"Put your dick away and let's go," Kash says from the doorway. "Cale called and said he needs us to hurry because Stone is getting more than his ass can handle. Hemy is there and about ready to take our fucking cash if we don't get there in ten."

I look away from the computer and stare his sweaty ass down. "So let him take my spot. Tell Cale I'll be there in an hour. I have something to do first."

Kash looks stressed as hell at the idea of telling Cale that I'm not coming in early. He grips the doorframe and huffs. "Just hurry the hell up. We might even need Hemy to stay after you get there."

"I'll be there." I write down the info I need and stand up, shoving the paper into my pocket. "You fuckers will be fine until I get there. Pull Kage onto the stage if you need to. He's been dying to dry hump the floor."

Kash just nods his head and takes off, running out the door, in a hurry to get to the club. He never wastes an opportunity to make money, especially when it involves women on his dick.

Grabbing my things, I lock the office door behind me and

quickly walk through the gym, making sure not to even look in the direction of any of the women here.

Every time I do, they expect me to take them back to my office and fuck them. It was fun in the beginning, but I'm over it. It was just something to pass the time and forget my worries for a while.

There would've never been anything more with any of them. Most of them came from *Walk Of Shame* and got memberships here, after they found out that I ran my uncle's gym on the side.

I've seen every single one of them all over Stone's and Kash's dicks as well as mine. I'm tired of women that will jump on the opportunity of taking any one of us to bed that shows them attention first.

I want a woman that is just about me and not all over my ass because of my occupation or because they see me as a hot fuck to brag about.

That's exactly why I'm headed where I am right now. I've waited to see Meadow show up at the club just for fun, but she hasn't. Which just proves that she was only there to find me to begin with.

If she was there for the entertainment, then she would've been back by now. I know . . . because the women I'm used to are always back the next fucking day. Once they come to the club, they become addicted to watching us and wanting us.

Pulling my motorcycle up to the address on Meadow's profile, I kill the engine and get off my bike.

My heart fucking goes crazy at the sight of Meadow standing on the porch, watching me, when I look up.

Her little tank top has my dick twitching as I take in her tits and tattoos.

She smiles big as I walk toward her, looking just as happy to see me as I am her. "I knew I should've put a fake address on that form," she teases. "Especially after seeing you that first night at the gym."

When I reach her, I cup her face and back her up against the door. "I would've found you anyway." Gripping her waist, I press my lips against hers, not being as gentle as the last time. I want her and I'm tired of holding back. "Trust me. When I want something as badly as I want you, I don't give up easily."

She pulls her bottom lip into her mouth as if my kiss hurt her. "Good," she whispers. "I'm tired of quitters. And men that give up because they find a new toy to play with. With all the toys you have around . . ." she looks up to meet my eyes. "I'm surprised you haven't already."

Her words anger me and something inside of me snaps. She thinks that she's just a fucking toy for me. She has no idea just how fucked up she's had me since day one. She's barely left my mind for longer than ten minutes. That's exactly why I'm here now. I've never gone to a woman's house because I needed to be with them as desperately as I do right now.

I grip her legs and pull them around my waist, pressing my erection against her pussy. "You really have no idea just how much I want you. If I didn't, then I wouldn't have waited until now to do what I'm about to do."

She grips the back of my hair and brushes her lips over mine. "And what is that?"

I smile against her lips. "*Fuck* you." I push the door open and begin carrying her through the house, until I find her bed. "Then I'm going to the club with you all over me because you're not just some play toy for me, dammit."

Tired of holding back, I toss her on the bed and rip her jeans down her legs, and then her panties, before flipping her over and slapping her ass, hard.

I wrap my fingers into the back of her long hair and pull as my other hand reaches around to grip her neck. I can feel myself breathing heavily against her ear. "I want you." I press my cock against her ass and then pull her up so that she can feel my heart racing against her back. "Can you feel how much?"

She nods her head and grips the blanket. "I want you too. Really fucking bad. I'm usually never like this with men. The way you have me thinking about you at all times."

With one hand, I push my jeans down my hips and pull out my cock, before slipping a condom on and taking in the sight of her beautiful ass and pussy.

"Damn, Meadow. That only turns me on more."

My need to be rough takes over and I feel myself losing control. I growl and push her head down into the mattress, before slapping her ass again and biting it.

She moans out as my tongue slides up her pussy, slowly and teasingly, before I stop and pull away. "Are you sure?"

"Yes," she breathes.

I spread her cheeks, my tongue working her pussy slowly at first, before I speed up and then dip my tongue inside of her.

She arches her back and moans out loudly as I slide my tongue in further, fucking her hard and deep with it, until I feel her shaking in my arms, close to losing it.

I lose all self-control, reaching around to grip her neck, hard, pulling her up flat against my chest. My hand squeezes, but I make sure to be gentle enough to let her know that I would never hurt her.

"Holy fuck . . ." I breathe. "I'll try not to be too rough, but I'm not sure that I can be gentle right now."

"Don't be." She grips the sheet and runs her tongue up my arm, before biting it. "Who says I like it gentle?"

"Fuck! I won't be then."

Sliding the tip of my dick across her entrance, I line it up just perfectly and then ease it in, before pulling out and slamming into her so hard that she bites down on my arm and screams.

She feels so good wrapped around my cock. I knew that she would, and not just physically. This is so much more to me right now.

Both of my arms wrap around her body, pulling her as closely as possible as I thrust into her repeatedly, wanting to show her just how much she gets to me.

She gets to me unlike any other woman ever has and I'm going to do everything to show her that.

I won't be stopping after tonight. She's not just a play toy for me. Fuck that shit.

"Oh fuuuuck!" I yell out, while picking her up and carrying her out of bed and over to the wall.

She grips my hair and moans out as I slam her against the wall and bury myself deep between her legs again. "Harder . . ." she growls against my lips. "Don't hold back, Styx. We both need this. I know you're not gentle. Let it out."

I push in deep and stop, making her scream into my arm and dig her nails in with each hard thrust after that.

I don't stop until she's shaking in my arms from her orgasm. I give her a few seconds to catch her breath. Then I walk her back over to the bed, lay her down and hold her legs over my shoulders, digging my fingers in as I fuck her deeper than I've ever fucked before.

Being inside her just doesn't feel like enough right now. I want to touch her in places that no other man ever has.

Gripping my neck, she pulls me down and presses her lips against mine, causing me to moan into her mouth as I come.

I'm so lost in the moment and this insanely beautiful woman, that I don't even bother pulling out. It's something that I always make sure to do, even though I always wear a condom.

With Meadow . . . I don't want to. I want her to feel what she does to me.

I pull her bottom lip into my mouth and gently suck it, before pulling away.

Then we both just lay in bed in silence, her head pressed against my chest.

I don't even know how much time passes, before my phone goes off and I come back to reality.

Groaning, I grab my phone, prepared to tell Kash to fuck off, but it's Cale instead. I can't be an asshole to him, even though I want nothing more than to stay right the fuck where I'm at.

"Fuck." I kiss her head and crawl out of bed. "I'm supposed to be at the club right now."

She looks up at me from the bed and even though she understands that I have to go, I feel guilty as shit for having to leave her.

I'm about to throw my shirt back on, but I find myself slipping it over her head instead and pulling her in for a kiss.

"I'll be back for this." I smirk. "Fuck it looks good on you."

She smiles back. "Is that your way of saying that I'll see you soon?"

I walk over to the door and stop to look back at her. "If I have it my way. Fuck yes."

"Good," she whispers.

Knowing that if I don't get out of here, that I'm going to end up saying fuck work and stay, I rush out of the house and jump on my bike.

Fuck . . . this woman has me. I know this now . . .

chapter TEN

Meadow

IT'S BEEN AN HOUR SINCE Styx left for the club and I'm still lying here in bed, wearing his cologne covered shirt.

This man does something to me that I just can't explain. When he showed up outside my house, unexpectedly, a rush of excitement and adrenaline coursed through me, making me feel alive with energy.

It's a feeling that I haven't gotten in a while. Something about Styx, makes me believe that there's something to look forward to. I've found that hope is something that I haven't felt since losing my aunt last year so this . . . it surprises me.

Everything that I have loved has been lost, starting with my parents and ending with the woman that raised me since the age of ten.

That's why I've put everything I have into the patients at the hospital, almost forgetting that I have a life myself. Any attachments outside of work has been impossible for me.

That's exactly why I need to be careful when it comes to

Styx. The sight of him in those perfect jeans, fitted tee and leather jacket does things to a woman's body and mind.

I lost all sense of thought as I watched him climb off his motorcycle and walk toward me with a confidence that only Styx seems to have.

I smile when I find myself sniffing his shirt. "There's something about you," I whisper. "And I think I want to find out just what that is."

Making a quick decision, before I can change my mind, I jump out of bed and gather some clothes to throw on. I must look like a hot mess right now, but I don't care.

I know that Styx was just here, but I haven't seen him in days and spending the little bit of time with him that I did, just wasn't enough. It only made me want more of him.

So much more.

Within thirty minutes, I find myself lining up outside *W.O.S*, looking around me at all the women that are waiting to get in.

There's got to be at least thirty women out here and who knows how many inside already, and almost every single one of them will be drooling over the man that I just had sex with and throwing money his way.

I've never felt anything like this before. It's exciting, yet strange at the same time, knowing that he could have any woman that he wants, but for some reason he's shown an interest in me.

I let out a flattered laugh and cross my arms, while waiting for the line to move. It seems to be taking forever and I can't tell if it's just because I'm anxious to see Styx or if it's because the line just isn't moving.

After about forty-five minutes of waiting in line, I look around me to see that the line hasn't moved much, since no one seems to want to leave to let others in.

"Crap!" Letting out a defeated breath, I turn around to leave, just to be stopped by strong arms encircling my waist and pulling me against a hard body.

"Miss me already?"

My heart races with that excitement that I only feel around Styx, as I turn around to look his sweaty body up and down. He's dressed in leather pants and *holy fuck* he looks dangerously sexy.

He's breathing heavily as he watches me check him out, taking in every glistening muscle. "I'm going to take that as a yes."

I laugh at his boldness and fight not to get lost in his insane blue eyes. "Maybe I was just bored," I tease.

Smirking, he steps up against me and wraps his hands into the back of my hair, before leaning in to press his lips against my ear. "I'll make sure to change that then."

Grabbing my hand, he pulls me though the crowd, nodding his head at the security guard, *Lane,* as we pass him to get inside.

The music is loud, the screaming of the women even louder than I remember it from last time.

And having everyone's eyes on me as Styx holds my hand has my body buzzing and my heart about ready to fly out of my chest with excitement.

"How did you know I was here?" I question close to his ear so that he can hear me over the noise.

"I didn't." He turns his face so that he's talking in my ear now. "I was *hoping.*"

The idea of him looking for me has me smiling so damn hard that it hurts. It only shows me that even with all these women around, I'm somehow still on his mind.

I get a little nervous when I realize that he's guiding me over to the VIP session where two beautiful women are sitting on the leather couch, talking and laughing.

They both look up once they notice me and Styx standing

in front of them, listening to their conversation about someone named Hemy.

"Woah," the blonde with tattoos says with a smirk. "Who is this hottie?"

Styx pulls me against him and grips my hip, possessively. "She's with me. Don't let any of the other assholes get too close."

The other girl lifts a brow and looks me over, smiling, as if she approves. "The guys get a little crazy here, so don't mind his manners." She grabs my hand and pulls me down to sit next to her. "I'm Sage and that's Onyx. You're good with us."

Styx laughs when I look up at him, confused. "They're with Stone and Hemy. My family will take good care of you when I can't. Just watch out for the blonde. She gets a little frisky."

Before I can say anything, he backs away and gets lost in the crowd of screaming women.

"He'll be back for you. I know that look." Onyx looks me over with curiosity. "I never thought I'd see the day that Styx brought a woman to us. I'm impressed. You're hot, babe."

I laugh and grab for the drink that Kage brings over to me. I remember him from last time and he seems to remember me since he brought me the same drink as before. "Thank you, Kage."

It looks like Kage is about to get ready to flirt, but Onyx shuts him down. "She's taken, dick head. Go pick one of the hundreds of other women in this room."

He laughs as she waves him off. "Hey, can't blame a man for trying."

The three of us watch as he makes his way through the crowd and picks out some random blonde to try his moves on.

"These fucking men of *Walk Of Shame*," Sage says with a smile. "Gotta love them all here."

My mind is still lost on what Onyx said before Kage came over.

"So should I feel special then?"

"You are," Sage says. "Styx doesn't just let *anyone* in. He seems to stick to himself."

My eyes seek him out in the crowd and lock on him once I find him grinding the stage and working it so damn good that even *I'm* sweating and completely turned on.

I don't even realize that I'm fanning myself off, until Sage laughs from beside me. "The boys know how to work it and they only seem to get *hotter* with each show."

Onyx grabs my hand and pulls it into her lap, while pointing across the room at a tall guy with long, dark hair, covered in tattoos. "That sexy as sin man over there is my husband Hemy. Trust me. Things only get better once they claim you as their own. What these girls get here at the club is just a glimpse into what these men can bring in the bedroom." She smiles. "Or the back of the club, pool, motorcycle or a friend's garage . . . wherever they want to take you."

My eyes widen as Hemy grabs the back of some girl's head and begins fucking her face. "And you're okay with that?"

Both the girls laugh, but it's Sage that speaks.

"When these men love, they love with everything in them. I have a feeling that Styx will do just the same. What they do here in the club won't even matter once you get to feel what they bring you both emotionally and physically outside of the club."

I sip my drink and bring my eyes back to Styx just in time to see him throw his pants off the stage and slide his hands into the front of his boxer briefs.

"I've already seen what that man can do outside of the club," I say mostly to myself. "I still haven't come down from that high."

Onyx finally releases my hand and smiles as Hemy walks up

the steps to where we are. "That's just the beginning, babe."

The way Hemy straddles her lap and grinds against her has my body heating up. It's as if he's fucking her right here next to me and they don't give two shits about who's watching them get off.

These men are too much to handle.

Holy fuck . . .

STYX

I CAN'T CONCENTRATE FOR SHIT, knowing that Meadow is here to see me. All it makes me want to do is spend all my fucking time on her.

If it weren't for the bachelorette party that Cale told me to focus on, I'd be over there right now, straddling her lap and whispering in her ear about just how damn beautiful she is and how I haven't stopped thinking about her since I left her house tonight.

My head has been all messed up since the moment I laid eyes on her at the gym and saw that there was something more to her than just a woman that wants to jump on my dick and take me for a test ride.

The way she looked at me, while I was buried between her thighs earlier, only confirmed that for me.

She's different than the rest.

Hands grab at me, pulling me in every direction, but I can't seem to pull my eyes away from Meadow sitting with the girls, talking and looking as if she's enjoying herself.

Every once in a while, when our eyes meet, she winks, letting me know that she's here for me.

"Fuck this," I growl out, unable to stay away anymore. My hands need to be on her fucking body.

I fight my way through the crowd of screaming women, not stopping until I have Meadow in my arms, her legs wrapping around my waist as I hold her up by her ass.

"I can't think straight with you in the same damn room." I run my mouth up her neck, stopping under her ear. "Do you know that? You're the only one that seems to matter when you're in the room. I would walk out right now just to spend time with you."

She grips my hair and pulls my head back to look me in the eyes. "I'll be here when you're done. I'm not going *anywhere*." Her lips curl into a smile. "I love watching you out there and I'm thinking I'd like to spend some time with you when you're done."

"Well, shit," I say with a grin. "Maybe I will just leave now. Take you back to my place and fuck you until you can't move."

I go to walk away, ready to carry Meadow out of here, but Hemy grabs my arm and stops me. "Your ass isn't going anywhere, fuck-tard." He looks around. "Not for a long fucking time. I'd like to take my woman home and bury myself between her fucking thighs too, but we have a job to do first."

Meadow brushes her lips over mine, when I don't make a move to release her. "Go," she whispers, before pulling my bottom lip into her mouth and then releasing it. "You're worth the wait."

Her words cause my heart to pound fast in my chest and before I know it, I'm carrying her through the crowd and grabbing a chair that Kash slides my way.

Forgetting that anyone else is in the room, I lower Meadow to the chair and straddle her lap, moving my hips to the slow rhythm.

My hands reach out to wrap into her soft hair and my lips are on hers without hesitation, showing the whole room that she's with me.

Any of these other fuckers in the room even think about touching her, I'll rip their throats out. Kage has barely taken his eyes off her since she walked into the room and I sent him to bring her a drink.

I'll fuck that giant motherfucker up if he lays one finger on her.

When I break away from the kiss, and pull Meadow to her feet, Kash walks over, half-naked, and presses his body behind her, picking her up so that her legs are around my shoulders.

Then he pulls her backwards so that she's hanging from my shoulders. The women go crazy as he takes her hands and runs them down his body, stopping above his dick.

I know what he's doing, because it was our plan to treat a woman to this, but I wasn't expecting it to be Meadow.

But knowing that her hands are running down his hard, sweaty body, has my blood boiling right now. It only gets worse when he grabs the back of her head and grinds his cock in her face.

It's the first time in my life that I've known what jealously feels like and it's a shitty fucking feeling.

I feel Meadow stiffen around my neck and grip my legs as if she wants me to pull her back up, so I back away from Kash and pull her back to me.

With my heart racing, I lower to my knees and lay her on the ground, before pinning her body beneath mine.

I grip her thigh with one hand, lifting it up so that I can push myself between her legs and line my cock up with the heat between her legs.

Her eyes meet mine the whole time and it's almost as if the

whole fucking room silences as I move my body against her to the slow beat.

It's not until Kash yells my name, that I come out of my head and run my hands through my wet hair.

I have no idea what the hell I'm doing right now, but I can tell that getting through the rest of this night is going to be harder than I imagined.

Grunting, I pick Meadow up, holding her close as I walk her through the crowd again and back over to the VIP section.

Both Onyx and Sage watch me with huge smiles as I lower Meadow to her feet and grab her hand, walking her over to sit back down in between them.

"Keep her safe for me. And tell Kage to keep his fucking eyes and dick in check."

Onyx grins and wraps her arm up in Meadow's. Hell, I might even have to worry about her ass trying to get close to my girl. "Oh, I'll keep her safe and comfortable next to me. No one with a dick will touch her." She winks, messing with me.

If she wasn't Hemy's girl, that fucker would kill me for even thinking it, I'd maybe even let her touch her as I watched.

'Cause I know after my cock, there's no way she'd want pussy over what I bring her in the bedroom.

But damn, if I don't want anyone touching her. Even Onyx.

Fuck . . . I need this night to be over.

chapter ELEVEN

Meadow

AFTER STYX GOT PULLED AWAY by Kash, he barely got another chance to come over to me.

I could see the exhaustion and need in his eyes, every time he looked over at me and all I could think about was doing something to make him feel good and let him know that I want to be close to him just as bad.

A part of me feels this need to let him know that I'm here for him and that someone else can take care of things for a while.

After the story he told me about his father, I get a feeling that he's spent a lot of his life taking care of others more than himself. He just carries so much on his shoulders and I can feel it.

"I'm going to find Styx."

Sage smiles and pulls me in close. "Check the showers. I have a feeling that you might find him in there. Just a little tip."

Onyx gives me a slap on the ass and winks at me. "Get it, girl and fuck the haters on the way."

Fixing my jeans, I walk through the crowd, holding my head

up high, when I feel eyes on me from all around.

Most of the women whisper shit, giving me looks as if they're judging me because of Styx's little display of affection toward me.

Well I say . . . fuck it. Onyx is right.

Walking faster, I search around me, stopping to ask one of the security guards where the showers are. He's so preoccupied with some chick, that he just nods his head toward the end of the hall and goes back to sucking on her neck.

"Thanks," I say to myself with a small smile.

Pushing the door open, I walk around to the showers to see Styx, standing there completely naked, dripping with water.

He looks rushed as if he has somewhere to be.

My eyes trail down his perfect, round, ass, watching the muscles in his legs flex as he pulls his jeans up.

"You should keep them off." I walk up behind him and wrap my arms around his wet body, before gripping the top of his jeans and tugging them down a bit. "They're just about as wet as I am right now."

His muscles flex beneath my fingers as he takes in a deep breath and releases it. "I wanted to catch you before you left."

I kiss his back, while gripping his jeans harder, pulling them back down his thick thighs. All I can think about right now is worshiping this beautiful as sin body. "I told you I wasn't going anywhere."

Rotating his shoulders, he cracks his neck and then slowly turns around to face me, completely naked, looking so damn beautiful and perfect that it's breathtaking.

His eyes lock on mine as he kicks his jeans away and watches me, waiting for what I'm going to do next.

Swallowing, I pull my eyes away from his and walk into the open shower stall, undressing and kicking my clothes out for

Styx to see.

The water barely turns on, before Styx appears in the doorway, watching with intense eyes. "Does being here make you feel dirty?"

I shake my head and reach out for his hand, pulling him into the water. "No. I don't think you got the shower you deserved after such a hard night's work. Let me take care of you."

Closing his eyes, he leans his head back and places his hands against the shower wall as I gently run my hands over his shoulders and then down his back.

"Fuck, your hands feel perfect on me."

I press my lips against his back as I reach for the soap and trail it over his tight muscles.

I've never showered with a man before and I have to admit that I'm extremely turned on, but . . . I want to let Styx know that this moment is more than that.

With soap, I work my way down his body, massaging his muscled legs with my hands.

He lets out a small moan of appreciation, leaning his head down into the water and just taking a moment to relax and enjoy the feel of my hands on him.

Holy hell, I'm enjoying it just as much.

"Turn around," I say in almost a whisper.

Taking his hands away from the wall, he turns around and faces me, his eyes admiring my body as I focus on cleaning his tattooed chest, before moving down to his abdomen.

"You don't have to do this, Meadow." He grips my hair tightly as I move down to his erection, moving my soapy hands over it. "I should be doing this for you."

"I haven't spent the whole night working hard. A woman shouldn't be the only one to be catered to. Hard working men deserve it just as much." I place my hand on his stomach and back him up against the shower wall. "Now close your eyes and enjoy."

Closing his eyes, he wraps his hands tighter into my hair, moaning as I stroke my hands over his dick, spending extra time on the head.

This man's body is so beautiful that I could spend all night doing this. He truly has no idea how easy it is to want to take care of him.

When his moans become louder, my movements pick up, knowing that he's getting close to coming.

"Come for me, Styx," I breathe, completely turned on and just as desperate for his release as he is. "All over my breasts. I want to feel you on me. Show me what I do to you."

His hands yank my head back and he growls out, shooting his come all over my breasts.

"Oh fuuuuuck." He looks down at me and massages his hands through my hair as the water washes over my breasts cleaning his release away. "Where the fuck have you been all my life? Stand up."

Pulling me up to my feet, he wraps his arms around me and holds me against him, under the water.

We stand here just letting the warm water pour down on us, not speaking for a while. We just take this moment to enjoy the feel of each other being close.

It feels good. So much better than I ever imagined and that scares me, but I don't want to leave.

After a while, he pulls away and presses his lips against mine. His lips are soft and smooth, yet his kiss is rough and firm, consuming me and making me want more of him.

Styx may be rough in the bed, but he has a gentle side. A gentle side that might just make me fall harder than I hoped.

His eyes meet mine. "Now It's my turn to take care of you."

Our lips meet again and he picks me up, wrapping my legs around his strong waist. I can feel his dick rubbing against my pussy and all I want is for him to fill me with it.

Breathing hard against my lips, he backs me up against the wall for extra support, as he slides his hand in between our bodies and fills me with his tattooed fingers.

He slowly pumps in and out, causing me to moan against his lips and grind my pussy, wanting him deeper.

The water drips down my lips to Styx's. With a growl, he sticks his tongue out, catching it in his mouth, before sucking my bottom lip and moving his fingers faster and harder.

My arm snakes around his neck, my other hand digging into his back, holding on for dear life as I moan out and begin shaking in his arms from my own release.

I can't even remember a time that I've had an orgasm so quickly in my entire life, but with this man, it's impossible not to.

After a few moments, he pulls his fingers out and sucks them into his mouth, before placing his forehead to mine.

"You have no idea how badly I wished that were my cock inside you instead." He gently bites my bottom lip, before releasing it. "You make me want more than just a quick fuck though. I want to spend my time on you, worshiping every inch of that beautiful body, until you fall asleep from exhaustion."

He slowly releases me, one leg at a time, helping me down to my feet, before turning off the water and walking out to bring me a towel.

"I hope like hell that I get that night soon."

I smile and reach for the towel, wrapping it around me.

When I step out of the shower stall, Kash is standing there naked, pulling his jeans up his legs.

The same damn sight I got when I walked in on Styx, except Kash is facing me, his dick standing at attention.

Swallowing, I quickly turn my head away, before I can spend too much time, admiring his insanely big dick and make this anymore awkward than it already is.

Styx smiles as if he's happy with how quick I was to turn away from Kash. Maybe he was expecting me to ogle over him like all the other women do.

When I turn back around, Kash is buttoning his jeans with a confident smile. "Sorry about that. I caught the end of your little shower date. Damn, that sounded hot as fuck."

My face heats up with embarrassment when I realize just how loud I was moaning while Styx was finger fucking me, just fifteen feet away from where Kash was changing.

The thought of someone possibly entering the locker room didn't even occur to me. All I could think about was taking care of Styx.

"Just hurry the fuck up, dick. You didn't have to sit around and wait for the ending," Styx snaps.

Kash looks me over in my towel, showing his appreciation. I can't deny that the way he looks at a woman heats you up in an instant. Those deep gray eyes do wonders. "No, but I wanted to." He winks at me and then grabs his shirt, walking out of the room.

Styx looks heated, his eyes watching the door as it closes behind him. "Let's get dressed so I can follow you home. It's late and I don't want you out there alone."

I reach for my clothes and quickly get dressed, before walking over to him and grabbing his face. As soon as his eyes look down to meet mine, my mind is made up. "Maybe you can stay."

The look in his eyes tells me that it's not a request that he usually even considers, but a part of him wants to right now.

"Let's go," is all he says, as he grabs my hand and walks me past some of staff and outside.

A group of women are waiting around the door, giggling and talking loudly about how hot each and every guy was tonight.

I'm hoping like hell that they're not waiting to suck Styx into their little group, because I honestly don't know what I'd do if he left me to hang with them.

I've had it happen to me in the past a few times, proving to me that the guy I was with really wasn't who I thought or hoped he'd would be.

Grabbing my hand, Styx speeds up, when one of the girls calls his name.

The tall brunette doesn't seem to want to give up. She calls his name a few more times, her friends joining in by whistling and yelling for him too.

I feel my face heating up with jealousy and anger that these damn women won't just give the hell up. Finally, I turn around and snap.

"Don't you see that he's leaving with someone. Get some fucking class."

I can barely finish what I'm saying, before Styx yanks me to him and starts making out with me, while walking me backwards into my truck.

"Get in and I'll follow you home," he says, between tugging on my bottom lip and sucking it into his mouth. "My motorcycle is across the lot."

I nod my head and jump inside my truck when he walks away. A few minutes later, he pulls up behind me and motions for me to drive.

I feel like an idiot the whole ride home and I have to admit that I'm disappointed in myself for even thinking a man like Styx would ever want to spend the night.

The only thing he made clear was that he was following me

home. That was probably his way of letting me down gently.

After I pull up at my house, Styx parks his motorcycle behind my truck, and gets off to meet me behind my vehicle.

He's silent the whole walk to the door of my house and surprises me when he walks inside behind me and locks the door.

I don't say a word as he follows me to my bedroom, undresses me and then does the same himself, before crawling into bed beside me.

Pinning my body beneath his, he reaches over to my nightstand and grabs my bottle of lotion, squirting it on his hands and rubbing them together. "Close your eyes and relax."

His naked body, above mine, has it almost impossible to relax, but I close my eyes anyway, moaning out as his hands rub over my body, massaging me.

Oh my God. How can he be so damn good with this hands? It's like every little touch from him is pure magic. Throw in him being naked and it's like a fantasy come to life. Getting a massage from a naked Styx is heaven.

Holy hell . . . I want this to last all night.

After he's done rubbing lotion over every inch of my body and making sure that I feel good, he spreads my legs open with his knee and lays in between them.

The feel of his erection brushing my entrance has me wanting to thrust my hips forward and hope like hell that he accidently pushes inside of me and continues to thrust.

"Fuck, Meadow. Don't move your hips like that. I'm trying my best not to casc inside of you right now and stay there all fucking night. I can feel the heat of your pussy tempting me. Fuck!"

The look in his eyes tells me that he's here for me. Not for sex. For me. And from what I can tell, that's new for him.

So I want the same.

I run my hands through his hair and pull him down to give him a gentle kiss on the lips, tugging on his lip as I pull away. "You make it hard to want to be good," I admit.

He moans against my neck and then rolls over beside me, pressing down on his erection. "Just wait until I get you alone again. Fuck. Come here."

The way his arms wrap around me and pull me close, says it all. I know because I feel the exact same way. Our hearts are racing and we can't seem to catch our breath in the darkness.

I want him here, but I'm scared of what can come out of it.

I'm scared of letting him in and us both getting hurt . . .

STYX

I WAKE UP TO AN empty bed, running my hands through my messy hair as I look around the small room.

Sleeping in a woman's bed isn't something that I do, yet I couldn't deny Meadow when she asked me to stay with her last night. Not after she stayed at the hospital to look after me.

What kind of a man would that make me?

I spent most of the night, holding her close to me and running my hands through her soft hair as she cuddled up on my chest.

Her naked body pressed against mine, her fingers tracing my chest and tattoos, it was a feeling that I welcomed and made me want to stay up even later so that I could enjoy it longer.

You better believe that I fell asleep with a boner and woke up to one, just thinking about our naked bodies being entwined.

Wanting to fuck her last night was one of the hardest cravings I've had to fight. This woman is making me fight myself and that's how I know that she's worth everything I plan to give her.

When I look beside me at the alarm clock, I see that it's past ten. Meadow's shift starts at eleven today, since she was asked to come in early, so I know that I'm alone in her house. She told me last night that she was taking on extra hours at the hospital this week.

"Well this is new . . ." Sitting up, I throw my legs over the side of the bed and run my hands over my face, before getting dressed and grabbing my things.

I walk through the kitchen to leave, but stop when I see a bright pink sticky note hanging from the microwave.

The smell of bacon hits my nose as I walk over and reach for the note to read it.

This is me saying thank you for last night.
~Meadow

"Well damn . . ." I can't help but to smile as I reach into the microwave and grab the plate of food out. I've never had a woman cook me breakfast before and I love that she thought of me this morning, before she left.

I don't usually eat when I first wake up, but knowing that Meadow took the time to cook me breakfast as a thank you, there's no way I'm leaving here without eating her meal. Every last bite of it.

I'll never do anything to disrespect her or make her feel bad or unappreciated.

My mother taught me that at a young age, although she doesn't seem to look for a guy with the same qualities, because she's still with my asshole father after twenty-four years.

Trying not to think about how much I miss her talks, I

quickly eat and send Meadow a text to thank her before heading home.

I'm surprised when I pull up on my motorcycle to see Kash's truck parked in my damn driveway. This isn't the first time.

"Well, fuck." Grunting, I slam my helmet down on the seat and walk to the door, pushing it open.

The first thing I see is Kash's naked ass, standing up on my couch, gripping some girl's hair, guiding her head up and down on his cock.

I chuck my keys at the back of his head, and he releases the girl's hair to rub the back of his head and scream. "Ouch! What the fuck!"

"Yeah exactly," I say pissed off, that he decided to have a little fuck-a-thon at my place without asking. "What the fuck are you doing here on my motherfucking couch?"

When he moves away from the girl, I see that it's Sophie, from the gym.

She smiles up at me, looking a bit embarrassed. Her dark hair is wild as shit and her eye makeup is thick and smeared across her face as if it's been a long night. "So this is where you live? I never thought I'd see it. It's nice."

Kash raises his brows and looks between the two of us as he sits down and covers his dick with his hands. "I should've known you two were pretty well acquainted. I did meet her at your gym and all." He smirks as if it doesn't bother him.

I didn't think it would. "You have your own place, fucker. I thought I took my key away the last time I caught your naked ass on my couch."

Grunting, I walk past them and into the kitchen to grab a beer. It's too early to deal with this crap. I need something so I don't flip my shit on him.

"My roommate trashed our place. Yours was cleaner." When

he enters the kitchen, he's dressed in the same pair of jeans that he left the club in last night.

"Yeah," I say, while looking him over, covered in sweat. "It *was* cleaner. Did you sleep here last night?"

He grabs a beer and pops the top. "Nah, we didn't sleep."

Sophie stands in the doorway half-dressed and looks us both over, with a look on her face, that's telling us exactly what she's imagining at the moment.

She wants to fuck us at the same time. That might've been something I'd agree to before, but it doesn't even sound appealing now.

"I've gotta go." She buttons up her blouse, trying hard to look sexy as she does. "My rides outside and I need some sleep before tonight. Later boys. I hope."

Kash winks and watches as she walks away, swaying her ass for us.

"What made your ass so sure that I wouldn't be home last night?"

He tilts back his beer and looks at me as if I've asked a stupid question. "After that shower, I knew it was different than your usual fuck. There's no way you weren't going home with her. I was in there for at least fifteen minutes before I even heard any moaning. It's usually within less than two seconds with us. I know how we work."

I look him over, letting his words sink in. That was definitely the first shower I've had with a woman that went like that. He's not wrong about that.

"You're steam cleaning my fucking couch today before work. I'm not touching it until you do. Your ass and dick are all over it."

"You even going to be here tonight?" he questions, watching me with a cocky smirk. "If not . . . then you might want me to wait until tomorrow to steam clean that shit. I have another date."

I set my beer down and run my hands through my hair, while making my way to the bathroom to shower, before I get the urge to break his pretty face. "Take care of that before tonight. I'll be staying here."

He laughs around his beer and then tilts it back. "Alright, man. Chill."

After I shower and get dressed, I leave Kash to take care of the couch, while I go out to the garage to do a little more work on my bike. It's still fucked up from my accident, but I'm slowly getting it back to how it was before.

Thirty minutes in and all I can think about is Meadow and how it felt, falling asleep with her in my arms.

I already miss the feel of her body against mine and the feel of her soft breath hitting against my chest as she fought to get as close to me as possible last night. Even in her damn sleep. It was like she couldn't get enough of me.

The thought of her against me has me hard. I can feel it straining against my fitted jeans.

"You working with a boner and shit?" Kash steps into the garage and laughs at my frustration. "You really have it bad for this girl. It's written all over your face, man."

"Maybe I do," I say mostly to myself. "So what."

He tosses me a beer and then opens one himself. "Leaves more women for me to fuck so no complaints from me, man. Just keep it separate from the club. If the women find out that two out of three of their favorite male entertainers are taken, then they're going to come less and spend less money. You know this. You've already given the damn crowd a show with her. You and fucking Stone are going to mess things up for the damn club."

I know Kash is right. Traffic slows down at the club each time one of us seems to commit, but that's the least of my concerns. I have enough money in my savings account to get me by for five fucking years without making another dime from the club.

If Cale has to replace me, then he has to replace me. He's a smart business man and knows what needs to be done. That's exactly why I love the guy so much.

"I gotta go." I stand up and slip my leather jacket on, once I realize that it's close to one.

Kash gives me a confused look and watches as I set the unopened beer down and toss my tools aside, before walking my bike outside of the garage. "Where you going? We don't work for another five hours."

"Somewhere I have to. Just lock up for me and I'll see you tonight."

"Alright, man. I got you."

Straddling my bike, I start it and take off down the road, my heart racing fast, just like it always does when I'm heading to this damn street.

So many thoughts and scenarios run through my head that I barely even remember driving there until I get to my destination and park.

Before I know it, I'm parked on the side of the road, down the street from my mother's house with my bike facing the direction that I know *he'll* be coming from.

I sit here and wait for twenty minutes, growing impatient and more on edge with each passing second that there's still no sign of my father.

He's late, which could be bad for my mother.

Finally, around one-forty he pulls into the driveway and gets out. He crosses his arms and looks my way, knowing that I'm here watching him. I always am now.

It only takes one look at my father to know whether or not he's wasted and it's usually after work that he would get fucked up and then come home to beat up on us.

That's exactly why, no matter what the fuck I'm doing, I stop and make sure that I'm here every single day when he gets off. And I will continue to do this until the day I know my mother is safe.

I want him to know that I'm watching him. He lays one finger on my mother again and his ass is mine. He may not walk again, the next time he hurts my mother.

I watch him carefully as he uncrosses his arms and then walks to the door, walking a straight line just to piss me off and show off.

He's sober. An asshole . . . but sober.

My eyes burn into his back, unwavering, until he's inside the house and the door is closed behind him.

Giving myself a second to cool off, I sit and just watch my mother's house to make sure there's no arguing or screaming coming from it.

When I feel safe to leave her alone with him, I start my bike and take off, heading toward my favorite burger joint.

I'm about three blocks from *Gill's Burgers* when I notice some asshole honking at cars and riding their asses as if he's in a hurry.

It only takes me a few seconds to realize that it's the asshole that hit me. I've been waiting to run into his ass again. "Oh fuck yes."

He turns down a side street so I speed up and turn down another side street, knowing that I'll meet up with him if I go fast enough.

I speed down three blocks and then turn left, blocking the

road at the next stop sign, right as he comes to a stop.

Adrenaline courses through me as I jump off my bike and take wide strides over to the driver side of the car. He looks at me with surprise as I reach into the window to turn off his car and snatch the keys out of the ignition.

The driver looks extremely worried now as he watches me grip the opened window and flex. "You're the asshole that hit me and you're still out here driving like a fucking idiot."

"Come on, man." He reaches out for his keys, but I snatch them away and shove them in my pocket. "Give me my fucking keys. Sorry, it was an accident. I didn't even see you there."

"Fuck that shit. You should learn how to drive or stay the fuck off the road, before you kill someone. Got it, asshole."

He looks me over with a cocky smile that shows me that he doesn't give a shit about what I'm saying right now.

The asshole has to be about eighteen or nineteen at most. So I'm sure he still gets off with a lot of warnings, but fuck that. Not with me.

I reach into the window and slam his head into the steering wheel as hard as I can. "I'll be watching you, asshole."

Turning around, I chuck his keys across the street and then hop back on my bike, revving the engine as he watches me through the windshield, while holding his nose.

He's lucky I didn't break it.

I feel a bit better and I find myself grinning like a fool as I pull up at the burger joint and order for two.

I have some thanking to do myself . . .

chapter THIRTEEN

Meadow

I CAN'T HELP BUT TO think that Jase has been keeping his eye on me extra closely over the last few days.

Every time I turn around, he's there asking me if I need something or if I want to go outside to his car and work off some steam. Seriously? I've worked with him for over a year and not once has he seemed so clingy until now.

At one point I might've wanted this kind of attention from him, but not anymore. Now that I'm getting it . . . it feels completely different than I expected.

Styx shows me attention in a way that makes me feel wanted and special. Jase has been showing me attention in a way that makes me feel smothered and annoyed as hell.

I hear something come from outside the door and immediately assume that it's Jase creeping around the corner to hit on me again. It's getting really damn old.

"I'm busy, Jase," I huff. "I've got patients to take care of and so do you. Leave me alone, please."

I inhale a deep breath and slowly release it when I hear the door to the room close and footsteps heading my way.

Fluffing up the pillow and getting the bed as comfortable as possible for the next patient, I speak, without turning around to face him. I'm not in the mood for his games and to be honest, he's sort of pissing me off at the moment.

I might just snap if I look at him.

Styx has been the only thing on my mind all day and Jase is ruining any quiet moment that I manage to get to think about what happened last night and remember just how good it felt to wake up with him in my bed.

He looked so damn sexy, laying there naked, wrapped up in my sheets and I want every second that I can get to picture just that.

"No, I won't go to your car with you and no, I won't take you to my truck."

Strong arms wrap around my waist, pulling me tightly against a hard body. His scent and the way he touches me, gives him away. "Then how about my motorcycle?"

Only Styx could make my heart beat the way it is at this very moment. I've learned that very quickly.

"What are you doing here?" I ask with a grin, while grabbing his arms. "Miss me already?" I tease.

He smiles against my neck, before tilting it to the side and gently biting it with his perfect mouth. "Maybe. Or maybe I got the feeling that you missed my mouth."

His hand lowers down the front of my scrubs and in between my legs, cupping me. "And my hands."

Biting my lower lip, I close my eyes and let out a small moan as he slips a finger inside and then pulls it out. "Your pussy definitely misses me, Meadow. Not sure I'll believe your mouth if it tells me no."

He turns me around and looks me in the eye as he sucks his finger into his mouth, tasting me. "Mmmm . . . My mouth misses everything on this perfect little body."

"Styx . . ." I breathe out, as he lowers down to this knees in front of me. "We can't do this right here." I grip his hair and tug when his warm mouth lowers down the front of my body, kissing me on the way as he lowers my panties. "A patient is . . . Oh my God . . . Styx . . ."

As soon as his tongue swirls around my clit, I lose all train of thought, gripping onto the bed railing for support.

His strong hands grip my thighs and squeeze as his mouth consumes my mind, body and soul, making it hard to think of the fact that we could get caught at any moment and I could possibly lose my job.

All that exists in this moment is Styx's tongue on my body, pleasuring me in a way that only Styx can.

"You took care of me at my work . . ." He stops to suck my clit into his mouth and swirl his tongue around it. It has me shaking above him. "Now I'm returning the favor."

Blindly, I struggle to lower the railing on the bed behind me, desperate for his mouth to keep going. "Move this . . ." I breathe out. "I need it gone. Now."

Styx smiles up at me, before reaching behind me and lowering the railing. Without saying a word, he grips my hips and raises me to the bed, pulling my ass to the very edge.

I lean back and grip his hair, wrapping my fingers in as he buries his face between my legs again.

With each swirl and flick of his tongue, I moan out, pulling his hair even harder. "Ohhhhh . . . shit . . . yes . . ."

My moans get louder, the more aggressively his mouth takes me and before I know it, I'm screaming out his name.

Styx laughs between my legs, before sitting up and covering

my mouth with his hand. "Try to hold it in. I'm not here to get you fired. I'm here to thank you."

I nod, and then push his head, until he's back down in between my legs. "Don't stop again or I'll hurt you."

I'm so lost in his mouth and the pleasure that it's bringing me, that I don't even notice the door to the room opening, until I hear Jase's voice as he walks inside.

"Hey, the patient is on his . . ."

"Oh shit! Dammit!" I sit up and push Styx's head away, just in time to see Jase stop in front of us with his mouth hanging open in shock.

Styx is quick to cover me up, making it clear that he doesn't want Jase seeing me with my pants down. "Fuuuck!"

He helps me to my feet and then runs his hands through his hair in frustration as he looks Jase over as he watches us.

"Are you fucking serious?" Jase clenches his jaw as he looks me over, clearly unhappy. "You *never* wanted to mess around in a room with me, but it's okay when this guy wants to? Suddenly, your job doesn't matter?"

"Jase- don't start," I growl out, frustrated that he had the nerve to bring *us* up.

Styx steps in between us, blocking Jase from looking at me as I quickly fix my hair and clothes, before smoothing out the bed. "Do we have a fucking problem here, Jase?"

He steps up close to his face, intimidating him. "If you even think about asking her to *your* fucking car again or to *her* fucking truck, I will hear about it and then you will hear from me. Got it? Don't fuck with what is mine."

My stomach fills with butterflies when I hear him say *mine* and I freeze. I don't know if he's just saying it to get Jase off my ass or if he really wants me as his, but holy shit, if those words didn't make my heart about beat out of my chest.

The boys step back and out of the way as the door opens and voices fill the room as Mandy and Julie help the patient to his bed.

Mandy stops to look at the three of us, before putting her professional face back on and making sure that the patient is comfortable.

I take this as my chance to grab Styx and get us the hell out of here, before anyone can ask any questions.

I know I'll have to explain to Mandy later, but right now, I just want an escape.

The look on Styx's face is mixed with anger and worry as he reaches behind the empty counter and picks up a brown paper bag.

"I brought you lunch. I didn't see anyone at the desk, so I left it here and looked for you." He wraps his arms around me and leans in to whisper in my ear. "Thank you for breakfast . . ." he lets out a sexy growl, causing goosebumps to cover my whole body. "And for dessert."

The worry on his face when he pulls away from me, causes my heart to drop. "Styx . . . I don't want anything to do with Jase anymore."

His eyes study mine, before he leans in and presses his lips against my forehead, kissing it gently. "He obviously doesn't get the picture . . . yet. Maybe I need to come around more."

He places the bag in my hand and flexes his jaw, while looking over my shoulder. "I'll be back when you get off work."

"Won't you be at the club?"

His blue eyes look down to meet mine and I can see the sincerity in them. "Yeah, after I make sure you get out of here safely. The club can wait."

"Meadow," the charge nurse calls out, sounding annoyed as usual. "You're needed in room 312. Please say goodbye to your friend."

Styx grabs the bag back out of my hand and sets it behind the counter again. "I'll see you tonight." He kisses me and then turns to walk away.

My eyes trail down this strong back, landing on his firm ass and I almost forget that I'm wanted, until Dani calls me again, letting me know that she's pissed.

Giving her a fake smile, I walk past her and disappear into room 312 to catch my breath.

The patient is sleeping, so I quickly do my job and then slip out the door, hoping that I can find a second to sneak into the bathroom and go over in my head what the hell just happened in that room with Styx.

I lock myself in the empty bathroom and lean against the wall, replaying Styx's mouth on me.

Holy fuck, I can't believe I just let him do that to me. Here. At work. I could've gotten caught.

I just hope like hell that Jase doesn't decide to be an asshole and get me fired.

After I have a few moments to myself, I step out of the bathroom just to have Jase waiting outside.

"What the fuck was that?" He follows beside me as I walk in an attempt to lose him. "You're fucking this guy over me? He's a male stripper. He doesn't even deserve your time, dammit."

"Fuck off, Jase." I stop abruptly and turn around to face him. "Don't you dare think that you have the right to judge Styx."

He laughs as if I just said something funny. "Styx. Real fucking nice. Sounds like a real man to me."

I shove my finger in his chest and dig it in as I look him in the eyes. "Oh he is," I say firmly. "More of a man than you'll ever be." My eyes trail down to his not so big bulge. "Styx seems to make every man other than him look small. Trust me."

"Oh come on. Don't do me like that." He follows me as I begin walking again. "Meadow . . . just let me take you out with me tonight. I'll show you what you've been missing. We'll have fun and you'll forget all about . . ."

He stops talking and lets out an angry grunt when I walk away from him to join Mandy and Dani as if he was never even talking to begin with.

This is going to be the longest day of my life . . .

chapter FOURTEEN

STYX

THE BRUNETTE DANCING IN FRONT of me, has been eye-fucking me ever since I walked out on that stage for my first performance. She's barely taken her eyes off me the whole night and it doesn't seem as if she plans to.

She's dressed in a short dress that barely covers her red thong and she keeps lifting it slightly in the front in an attempt to get my attention.

It's been working, but not in the way I'm sure she hopes for.

Kash appears next to me, out of breath as he watches the way she's watching me as if she wants to tear me apart with her teeth.

He slaps my back and chuckles. "You going to give her what she wants, man? She's been working all damn night to get your attention. I've never seen so much desperation in my damn life."

I reach up and wipe the sweat off my forehead, while pulling my jeans back up my hips. "No. I'm good."

Breathing heavily, I rush past the herd of women and over to the bar, grabbing the beer from Sara as she slides it my way with a crazy smirk.

Tonight has been total insanity and I've been completely distracted with keeping my eye on the clock and trying to avoid my stalker for the night. I told Meadow I was meeting her after her shift and I plan to be there no matter what it takes.

I keep my word.

Walk Of Shame will have to wait.

I've never been late when my father gets off work and I won't be for Meadow neither.

"Woah there, gorgeous. Looking a little sweaty. Your stalker wearing you out already? Want me to get the water pitcher to cool you off?" She winks and laughs as I tilt the beer back and then pour some over my head to cool off.

I'm that damn hot.

Her throwing water on us is the highlight of her damn night. She did it once a few months back and now it's become almost a nightly routine.

Sometimes just to fuck with us, she throws some ice in it. That's why you want to keep on her good side. Ice does not do the body good. Especially the most important part and the way she's looking at me now gives me the idea that there'd be ice in my pitcher for annoying her.

"Nope, I got it. What time is it?"

"Someone sure has been asking about the time an awful lot tonight. What . . . Do you think I don't have better things to do than check the time every twenty minutes for your ass?" She walks over to the register to grab her phone with a roll of her eyes. "It's a quarter to eleven. Why? It's not like-"

"Shit." I slam my empty beer down on the bar in front of her when she walks back over. "Tell Cale I'll be back in thirty. I gotta go take care of something important."

"Styx," she yells after me, when I take off through the crowd in a hurry. "What the hell. You're in the middle of a damn show."

"Was!" I yell back, before pushing past Lane and out the back door, shirtless with my jeans still unbuttoned.

Grabbing my helmet, I straddle my bike and rev the engine, ignoring Lane's attempts to get my attention.

I'm just about to speed off, when I feel a hand run down my bare back. "Where you headed, Styx? I can be some pretty good company."

Growling under my breath, I let out a frustrated breath and shake my head as the tall brunette walks around me, trailing her hand along my body on the way.

This is exactly why I'm done with the girls that come to the club. They're all the same and it doesn't amuse me anymore.

"I'd love for you to take me for a ride. Ever fucked on a motorcycle?"

She lifts the front of her short dress and slides her hand inside her panties as if that's the key to getting me where she wants me.

"Yes," I say stiffly, while pulling her other hand away right as she goes to reach for my package. "But I won't be fucking *you* on *mine*."

Her face looks shocked as she scans my body over with hard eyes. "Seriously? You're saying no? To this . . ."

I look down at her hand as she begins pumping her finger in and out of her pussy and moaning.

That shit isn't working on me. I'm not even fucking hard.

"Fuck yes I am."

Before she can say anything else, I speed out of the parking lot and toward the hospital, not the least bit affected by her attempt to fuck me.

I've had hundreds of girls just like her throwing themselves at me since I started stripping at the club. It takes much more to hold my attention now.

Even though it's dark, I catch heads turning my way, but I ignore them all, until I'm pulling up next to Meadow's truck.

I park behind it and get off my bike to lean against her vehicle and wait. Running my fingers through my hair, I realize just how sticky I am from that beer.

Maybe I should've let Sara pour that pitcher on me. Holy fuck this does not feel good right now, but I didn't want the ice that was sure to be in that pitcher.

I'm not even waiting for five minutes, when I look up to see Meadow watching me with surprise in her eyes.

It's as if she didn't believe I'd really be here. I hate the idea of that.

"You made it. Shirtless . . . but you made it." She smiles and walks toward me, stopping a few inches in front of me. Her eyes lower down to my bare chest, before raising back up to meet mine. "You really didn't have to leave work for me. All those screaming women back at the club paying to see the sexy, shirtless man in front of me and you still came to see me?" she teases. "I'm shocked you even remembered my name, Styx."

My eyes drift a few parking spots over, locking on Jase. He unlocks his Mustang, keeping his brooding eyes on me the whole time as he opens the door, making it clear that he's watching us.

"I always keep my word and I'll never forget your name," I say stiffly, to let Jase know that I plan on sticking around for a while. "What are your plans for tonight?"

I shouldn't be asking her this, but seeing the look in her eyes when she first saw me standing here, makes it impossible for me not to want to spend time with her right now.

Going back to the club to dance for other women is the last thing on my mind. I can't. So fuck it.

"My plan was to go home and watch . . ."

Jase pulls up behind us, rolling down his window and interrupting what Meadow was about to say.

"Everything okay out there, babe? Sure you don't want to take me up on that offer from earlier? We can pick up your car in the morning. It'll be fine here."

Instinctively, my arm wraps around Meadow's waist and I hold her close as she responds to the douchebag.

"Firstly . . . I'm not your babe. Don't call me that again. Secondly . . . I already told you to fuck off. Goodnight, Jase."

Grunting, he gives me a dirty look and speeds off, doing a burnout as if that shit is going to intimidate me.

Meadow is distracted with watching him, so I flip her around and press her against her truck.

I can't help but to notice the way my heart speeds up as soon as our bodies meet. "Did he mess with you today?"

She leans her head back, resting it in my hand, as she looks up at me. "Doesn't matter. I took care of him. It's fine."

Hearing that pisses me the hell off, but there's nothing I can do now that he's gone. I'll have to deal with him later. "You've had a long night at work." I lean in and whisper in her ear. "Follow me."

I really need to take care of her right now . . .

chapter FIFTEEN

Meadow

MY HEART IS RACING THE whole time that I'm following Styx to his house. At least I think that's where I'm following him.

I didn't ask any questions. I didn't feel the need to. He asked me to follow him and my entire body gave me no other choice but to listen.

He keeps surprising me and I have to admit that I love that.

I never actually expected him to leave work and show back up at the hospital like he said. I've become used to words with little action to back them up when it comes to men.

At least the one I trusted the most. He left me at my worst and I still haven't forgotten.

Styx is proving to be different and with each word that leaves his mouth, I find myself becoming more and more attracted to him and not just physically.

I feel a pull toward him that no other man has been able to make me feel since I've closed myself off ten months ago.

Not to mention that the way he looked at Jase in the parking lot was as if he wanted nothing more than to protect me from him and I have to admit that I loved it more than I expected. It made me feel safe and wanted.

A feeling that I miss with everything in me.

My heart continues to race as I pull up in the driveway beside Styx's motorcycle and unfasten my seatbelt.

I have no idea what he has in mind for us tonight, but I'm dying to find out. Spending time with him is something that I seem to look more forward to with each passing day.

Before I get a chance to even reach over and grab my purse from the passenger seat, my truck door flies open and Styx reaches in to pull me out.

The way he handles me is a complete turn on and I instantly think about sex with him, making me want him again. Once was not enough.

His blue eyes meet mine as he slams my truck door shut and lifts me up, pushing me against the side of my truck with his hips. "I've been thinking about taking care of you all night. There's so many dirty things I want to do to you right now, but I won't. You deserve so much more. You give so much to others. Let me *give* to you."

He closes his eyes and then leans in to kiss my neck, moaning against me. The vibration of his mouth against me has me moaning out load and closing my eyes in enjoyment. "Maybe I want both sides of you, Styx. The caring and the *dirty*. Maybe I want the dirty right now. Maybe I *need* it."

He growls against my neck and then bites it, brushing my skin with his rough beard as he moves. I love the feel of his beard on me. So damn hot. He's not making it any easier to wait. "I won't touch you while I have other women on me, Meadow. I need to take care of you first."

He begins pulling me away from the truck, but I yank his

hair, letting him know that I'm not ready to go in yet.

It's dark and quiet out here. Maybe people are awake . . . maybe they aren't. Doesn't matter. I want him. Right. Now.

"Wait . . ."

He stops walking at the sound of my voice, giving me a curious look. "Everything okay?"

I reach in between us and rub my hand over his thick erection, showing him that everything is more than okay. "I just don't want to go inside yet."

He has me completely turned on right now and it makes me want to try something that every guy I have been with before has been afraid of doing. The idea of this has always gotten me excited.

He smirks down at me once he realizes what I'm asking him to do. "Right fucking here? We'll wake the whole neighborhood."

I nod my head and squeeze his dick through his pants. "I don't care. Let us wake them then."

My words cause him to rush to the back of my truck and pull the tailgate down, setting me down inside.

Holy shit, this is really about to happen.

With his eyes burning into me, he grips my hips with force and pulls me down to the edge of the truck bed so my ass is barely hanging on the surface.

Keeping his intense eyes on mine, he pulls my scrubs down my legs, tossing them aside as he admires my body with a moan of appreciation.

His hands roam up my legs and thighs, giving me chills.

Before I can even register what he's doing, he has my thong in his hands, ripping them from my body with a growl.

My legs tremble with excitement and anticipation of him taking me hard, and I find myself unable to wait. I'm too damn turned on now.

"I need you naked, Styx. Holy shit, you're so damn sexy."

A soft rumble comes from his throat as he quirks an eyebrow and grips both of my wrists in his hands, pulling me up to meet his jeans. "You want me naked," he whispers. "Show everyone how badly. Undress me . . ."

Biting my bottom lip, I unbutton his jeans and yank them down with force, along with his briefs, my eyes taking in every inch of his perfection. And trust me, there's a lot of inches to take in.

I notice him struggling to reach into his jeans, before he kicks them aside and rips the wrapper of a condom open with his teeth.

My eyes are on his perfect mouth, but lower when he struggles to roll the condom over his erection.

He strokes his lengths a few times, watching as I yank my shirt off over my head and toss it aside, waiting for him to take me how I want him right now.

"Fuck me!" Gripping my thighs, he steps in between them and slams into me, hard.

I scream out while wrapping my legs around his waist, causing him to thrust harder, rolling his hips in and out in perfect rhythm.

My grip on his bicep, tightens, me wanting him harder and faster. I can't get enough of this man right now and I want him to feel this.

With each hard thrust, I scream out and dig my nails into his skin, only making him go harder and deeper, until we're both moaning out our pleasure, him coming right after I squeeze him tight.

"Fucking shit," Styx breathes against my lips. "I wanted to take care of you first. I'm dirty and sticky from the club, but I can't deny you of shit."

I laugh and suck his lip into my mouth, biting it gently, before releasing it. "I couldn't wait. I've been thinking about touching you all day."

Pulling me away from the truck, he walks us toward his opened garage, fisting my hair with his free hand as I straddle his waist and hold on tight.

The garage door closes behind us and I find myself melting into Styx as he walks us through the house and to the bathroom.

Opening the glass door, he reaches in and turns on the shower water, before setting me down to my feet and pulling his condom off, tossing it outside of the shower. "You've had a long night at work now let me fucking take care of you."

He begins stripping my bra off and all I can think about is the fact that he should be at work, yet here he is, catering to me. He lowers down to his knees, running his hands up my legs.

"Styx . . ." I grab his hair and meet his gaze. "Shouldn't you be going back to the club? I don't want you losing your job over me."

He shakes his head and kisses up my thigh, stopping before he gets where I want him. "I'm not going back tonight. Forget about the club. It doesn't matter right now. I'm here with you. You matter."

Butterflies fill my stomach and a happiness that I haven't felt in a long time has me smiling so hard that I can't fight it.

What is this man doing to me?

I step under the water and close my eyes as the warmness runs over my skin, relaxing me. He's right. It's been an extremely long day at the hospital and I need this right now.

His hands rubbing soap over my skin, his lips kissing me in places that gives my whole body goosebumps. I need this.

He's gentle in the way he touches me now. The way he washes my hair. The way he massages the thick soap into my shoulders, making my whole body feel so damn good.

I lean into his hard body as his hands snake around the front of me, rubbing soap over my hard nipples, before disappearing between my legs.

One hand pushes my legs apart, while his other hand brushes over my sensitive pussy, making my body crave for him to take me again.

"Styx," I moan out. "I love the way you touch me. I might get too used to this if you keep being so damn good at it."

He stops just long enough to dip a finger inside me, before he goes back to rubbing my clit with his other fingers. "Maybe I want you to get too used it. Maybe I want you to be familiar with my touch," he whispers from behind me. "So if another man touches you, you'll crave for the familiarity of my fingers pleasing you and making you come undone."

I lean my head back and cry out as his movements speed up and his erection presses against my ass, teasing me. "Maybe I like the idea of you coming undone only for me . . ."

As soon as his teeth dig into my neck, I come undone under his touch, gripping onto his arm as my orgasm rides out.

"Hooooly fuuuck . . ." I breathe into his arm and squeeze it. "It's like you know exactly what I need and you give it to me, but even better."

He laughs into the top of my hair. "Is that why you stalked me at the club that first night? Just one look at me and you knew I'd be damn good at pleasing you."

I teasingly bite his arm and laugh. "You like the idea of me stalking you so much, that you decided to stalk me back, Styx Sterling."

He holds onto me with one hand and reaches for the soap to rub down his own body now. "You like me so much that you've learned my last name." He stops and turns me around to kiss me. "Fuck, I love that," he whispers against my lips.

"Good," I whisper back, before jumping up and wrapping my legs around his waist. "You know what I love?"

"Tell me," he growls, before biting my lower lip.

"When you make me feel wanted and protected." I press my lips to his, while reaching behind him and turning off the shower water. "The way you held me the other night. The way you kiss me. The way you touch me and the way you fuck me. I could keep going on."

He grips my ass and bites my bottom lip again, but harder this time. "Fuck, I want to keep you."

I smile against his lips. "After that delicious burger you brought to me for lunch today, I might want to keep you too. We'll see . . ."

He laughs and then kisses me. "Let's get you to bed. You can hardly keep your eyes open."

Holding onto him, I bury my face into his neck, taking in his sexy scent as he carries me through his house and to his bed.

If I weren't so exhausted right now, I'd ride this man all night, just to listen to him moan, while he's inside me.

Everything about Styx turns me on and makes me desperately want him right now, but a twelve-hour day dealing with sick patients has taken its toll. Once will have to be enough for tonight.

I feel myself falling asleep right when he snuggles in behind me and pulls the blanket around us.

I'm beginning to love this feeling way too much . . .

STYX

I WAKE UP TO THE sound of something vibrating from the bathroom floor. It takes about the third time, before I finally shake my sleep off enough to realize that it's my phone.

My jeans are still on the bathroom from when I fetched them from outside, right before crawling back into bed with Meadow.

"Fucking shit." Being careful not to wake Meadow, I slip out of my bed and rush to the bathroom, grabbing my phone right as it goes off for the fourth time.

"What the fuck, Styx." Cale's angry voice comes through the phone, making me feel instant guilt for not coming back to finish my shift like I told Sara to tell him I would.

I've only ever heard Cale angry once. It takes a lot to piss him off and I'm an asshole for being the reason for it now.

I let out a long breath and run my hand through my hair. "Shit. I'm an asshole. I'm sorry, man. It won't happen again."

"I can't just have you leaving the club during the middle of a damn show like that. I understand that Sara said it was important, but you need to talk to *me* and let *me* know that. I have no problem calling in Hemy or looking for an extra dancer to fill in so you can have more time off. But fucking tell me. Got it?"

"I'm sorry, man. I planned on coming back, but then I couldn't leave her once I saw her. She's in my bed right now. Want me to come in for the last thirty minutes and do a couple songs?"

He's silent for a few seconds, before responding. "Damn, Styx." He laughs into the phone as if he's relieved. "All this time I was thinking you were in some kind of trouble with the way you've been acting lately. I should've guessed it was a woman."

"This is new to me, Cale. I'm doing my best to show her that I'm more than just a male entertainer that sleeps around for fucking fun. She's different . . ."

"Good. Because I'm giving you the next two nights off. Take her out on a real fucking date, Styx. Not just to the bedroom or the kitchen counter or wherever it is that you usually take her."

I smirk into the phone. "That was my plan."

"I need your head in the game on Friday when you come back. But just remember that the next time your ass leaves me hanging; I'll have to fuck you up. Better yet, I'll get Slade to do my dirty work. That fucker is always looking for a reason to slip out of his suit for a day."

We both laugh at his fake threat and then hang up.

When I walk back into the bedroom, Meadow is spread out on my bed. She smiles up at me and motions for me to come to her.

"You're so fucking sexy right now." I crawl above her and lean down to suck her bottom lip into my mouth. "I'll never get used to the way my heart jumps whenever I touch you." I suck her bottom lip into my mouth again, before releasing it. "Or my cock."

Moaning out, she bites my bottom lip and tugs, pulling me back down to her. "I want you inside me, Styx. I haven't been able to stop thinking about the truck how damn good you felt. Think you have another round in you?"

I wrap her hair in my hand, before reaching over to my nightstand and grabbing inside for a condom. "After this, I don't think you'll be asking that question *ever* again."

Once I get the condom on, I stand on my knees and look down at her, while grabbing her ankles, and placing them on my shoulders. "I should be asking you if you think you can handle another round. I always have another round in me. For you, I fucking have ten if that's what you want."

I position myself between her legs and enter her in one thrust. We both moan out as I hit hard. I don't think I've ever been so damn deep before.

I begin to move in a slow, steady rhythm before speeding up, causing her to slam her head into the headboard. She throws her hands behind her and pushes off of the bed as I continue to take her, hard and deep.

She's watching the way my body moves as if she's hypnotized by it and can't get enough of it. "I've never seen a man move his body as damn sexy as you do," she whispers.

I lean into her lips and whisper, "You like watching me move, baby? Does it feel as good as it looks?"

She nods her head and moans out as I slam into her and rotate my hips. "So much better. You feel better. Nothing is more real than that."

Her lips crush mine and she digs into my back as I push in deep and stop, us both breathing into each other's mouths. "You feel so good wrapped around me. I could do this all fucking night if you'd let me."

"Then do it," she growls against my mouth.

And I do.

Until we're both exhausted and our muscles are shaking.

It's been a while since I've gotten into the gym, but fuck me, this was just the workout I needed.

I'll do this, every night with her if she'll let my ass.

And I have a feeling that she'll be able to keep up . . .

AFTER MEADOW LEFT THIS MORNING to meet up with her friend Mandy, I headed to the gym to get a workout in and meet up with my uncle Wes.

We've spent the morning signing all the necessary papers to make the gym mine and catching up since he hasn't stopped in for months.

"I can't believe that I'm giving this damn place up," he says with slight sadness in his voice as he looks around his old office. "It took me years to save up for this place, but family is where it's at, Styx. Never forget that shit. Your father . . . well he's a piece of shit and never learned the meaning."

I toss my pen aside and look across the desk at my uncle. I actually take a lot more after him than I do my father, thank fucking goodness. "Oh, you don't have to tell me that shit. I learned that at a young age. I hate that son of a bitch. Always will. He's no father. Never has been."

"Too fucking bad too. How's Lily doing? Dana hasn't heard from her in weeks. Should we be worried or are you still checking up on her every day?"

"You know I am. And I will for as long as I have to until she leaves that piece of shit."

My uncle looks at me with a smile, before standing up and gripping my shoulder. "I don't give a shit what anyone says, I'm proud of you. Fuck what your father says about you being a male entertainer. You're young still and you should live a little. But you've got your head on right and you know what's important. You just need to find it still. That's why I trust you with this gym. It's the one thing that I know you love."

I stand up and throw an arm around him, letting him know that I appreciate his words. "Thanks, man. I don't know what I would've done without you over the years."

"Well you'd be a male stripper of course." He raises a brow and smiles. "But you wouldn't have a gym."

I smile back and start cleaning my desk off. "Can't argue that. And I love your ass for it too."

He walks away to leave, but stops at the door and turns back to face me. "Love your ass too. Tell your mom hi for me and that she needs to call us once in a damn while. Or at least answer the phone more."

"I will. Now get out of here so you can get on the road with your family. I'll come visit when you guys get back."

"Alright, man. I'll you see you later."

"Later, Wes."

After my uncle leaves, I sit back down at my desk and look around the office, feeling proud as fuck to be the owner of this gym. I've spent the last four years practically running it and putting my time into it.

What I'm dreading is the talk with Cale, letting him know that I'm going to have to cut it down to two days a week at the club.

I want to make sure that I'm here more for my staff and members. I haven't been able to do that with the club being so busy for the last two months.

I hear a knock at my door, before Slade lets himself in and takes a seat at my desk, dressed in that fancy ass button down and slacks that he sports now that he's a lawyer again.

He grins and tosses a *Walk Of Shame* flyer my way. "Shit, I don't miss going to that place and shaking my cock for hundreds of screeching women."

I get comfortable in my seat and look him over. He's gotten bigger since last time. It's been months since I've seen him. I used to see him at least two times a week, but my schedule has had me all messed up and tired.

"Fuck . . . your ass has gotten big. I see you've been here almost every day after work now. Everything good with Aspen?"

He laughs as if I just asked a stupid question. Hell, it was a stupid question.

"Don't ask me that shit again. Things will always be good with Aspen. How about you, dick? Cale tells me that your head hasn't been into the club lately."

I laugh. "Is this him sending you to fuck me up?"

Watching me, he begins rolling up the sleeve of his black shirt, revealing his tattoos. "Nah, I'm not trying to fuck up my new shirt." He smirks, looking confident and cool as usual. "I just wanted to check on you and make sure that you're good. I know how the stress of the club can get to you."

I take a deep breath and release it, while sitting back in my chair. "I guess I'm just tired of the same old shit. I work my ass off there and every single girl expects me to take them home and fuck them. I'm over it."

"Hell, the Styx I met over a year ago was into that shit. I was too in the beginning, but fucking just for the fuck of it gets old. I want to fuck because I want to hear the woman below me scream that she fucking loves me and no other man. Not because I want to pretend that love doesn't exist and fucking is just a way to forget. It took me a while to figure it out, but I did with Aspen. Leaving the club and that lifestyle behind was the best decision of my life."

I take his words in and my whole body aches to feel that with Meadow someday. For too long, I have been fucking just to forget all of the other shit in my life that sucks, and telling myself that I'll never find the right woman to change that.

But Meadows different. I'm different with her.

"I've been thinking about leaving the club," I confess. "That place has fucked with my head for too long and I want to focus on my gym and Meadow. I can't do that when I have to spend my nights there, pleasing other women."

Slade sits up straight and gives me a questionable look, while loosening his tie. "Woah. Back the fuck up. Who the hell is Meadow?"

The sound of her name coming from his mouth has excitement coursing through me. Damn, this woman has me all fucked up over her.

"Hopefully mine soon. That's who."

"Well damn . . . I know that look, man. You have it bad for this woman. I know because I gave every other fucker that look when they asked me about Aspen. She was mine and I needed everyone to know." He stands up and reaches into his pocket when it starts vibrating. "I need to get back to the office for a meeting. I'm already late. Talk to Cale and tell him what you want. He'll understand. Plus, there's plenty of male entertainers banging down the door of *WOS* to get on that stage and make money. He'll be fine and so will Stone and Kash. Don't let that shit stress you out and force you into staying."

Standing up, I shake his hand and thank him, before he walks away and answers his phone.

Once he's gone, all I can think about is what he said. Maybe he's right. Maybe I need to have this talk with Cale. But that's not the only thing he's right about. I do have it bad for Meadow. Way more than I fucking know.

I pick up my phone and send Meadow a text.

Styx: I want to take you out to dinner tonight. Wear something dressy. Or hell. Anything you want.

She responds a few minutes later, causing my dick to get hard and my heart to beat fast in my damn chest.

Meadow: I'll wear nothing if you want me to and we can even stay in at your house. I just want to spend time with you.

"Holy fuck, this woman is perfect for me."

Now, I just want this day to hurry the hell up so I can make it to her, but I have a lot to do here first.

Just when I think I'm about to have a few minutes to myself after a long day here at the gym, James lets himself in and walks over to take a seat at my desk. He smiles and then reaches over to shake my hand. "Hell yes. Congratulations on being the owner of this badass gym. Of course, a lot of it has to do with me being here." He flashes a cocky smile as I reach out for his hand and shake it.

"You are as cocky as you fucking look, dipshit." I mutter. "What do you want?"

He stands when I do. "I need to leave early tonight. I have a date. Is that cool?"

"Yeah, man. Ben can handle it. Just let him know that you're leaving early."

"Hell yes!" He does a little dance, similar to some shit that I'd pull at the club. He's actually pretty good too.

"Did you steal that shit from me?" I joke. "Stay away from the club, fucker and don't use my moves on your date."

He winks and dances his way out of my office, shutting the door behind him.

That fucking kid is something else.

Now to give Meadow the night that she deserves . . .

chapter SEVENTEEN

STYX

I'M SURPRISED WHEN I PULL up at my house to see my mother sitting on my porch with her head down.

Instantly, I assume the worst and thoughts of me kicking that son of a bitch's ass take over.

I barely even park my bike, before I jump off and run over to her, grabbing her face to look for bruises. "What did that asshole do now? Did he hurt you again?"

She laughs and grabs my hands, pulling them away from her face. "Sit down for a minute. Don't let yourself get so worked up, baby. I'm fine." Sternly, she points to the empty space next to her. "Sit and relax."

I release a breath and take a seat, fucking relieved that I won't have to kill that bastard today. He's lucky . . . for now. "Are you really okay? Don't lie to me. Don't ever lie to me to protect him. Got it?"

Smiling, she leans in close and rests her head against my shoulder. "I'm fine. I just missed my baby boy. You haven't been by to see me in almost three weeks. I wanted to make sure *you* were okay. Are you?"

I feel like shit, the instant she points out my neglect for the last few weeks, but she knows more than anyone why I haven't gone inside to see her. I'm usually sleeping or at the gym when he's gone at work and when he's there it always turns into a fight and I'm to that point where I know I won't be able to control myself when it comes to him.

"I'm fine. You're more than welcome at my house, mom and you know it. I'm always here for you, but I can't look at that piece of shit. I'll kill him if I see any more bruises on you. I can't do it anymore. We've put up with his shit for too long. I just wish you could see that. He's not worth your time and effort."

She lets out a small sigh and holds onto my arm as if she doesn't want to let go. "You're the best son any mother could ask for, but I just need you to come over once in a while and see me. We all need to move on from the past. Please . . . just do this for me. Your father has been going to counseling and he isn't the same he was six months ago. If we treat him like he is, then he might as well still be. Right?"

I close my eyes and pinch the top of my nose. She's asking a lot of me with this. I'll never forget or forgive the shit he's put us through. I can't.

How can you just sit in a room with a monster and pretend that he isn't the evil that ruined everything you loved growing up?

I can't answer that, but for my mother, I'll do anything, no matter how much it hurts me.

"When do you want me over? I'll do dinner, but I can't do a poker night where he's drinking all night and acting a fool. I'll be gone before that. It'll only stress me out and have me hounding his ass to make sure he doesn't get out of control."

"Tomorrow night. I'll cook your favorite meal and your father will be on his best behavior. I promise. He already knows I'm here asking you and he's promised to behave and not give you a hard time."

I sit for a few seconds, considering her offer, when my phone vibrates in my pocket. The idea that it could be Meadow, has me reaching in my pocket for it and unlocking the screen.

My mom looks down at my phone and smiles. "Who's Meadow? Do you have a girlfriend that you're keeping from me? Styx." She playfully pushes my shoulder and laughs.

My heart speeds up with excitement as I scan over the message. I can barely hide the smile that takes over as my mother watches my face as I read the message.

It's probably been forever since my mom has seen me as happy as I feel right now with this damn phone in my hand.

> *Meadow: I wanted to let you know that I'm home and ready when you are. Can't wait to see you tonight.*

I don't even realize that my mother is reading over my shoulder, until she grips my arm in excitement and squeals. "I need to meet this Meadow. Ask her to come to dinner tomorrow night for tacos. It'll be fun. I promise."

The thought of bringing her around my father has my heart sinking and my stomach twisting up in knots.

"Not a good idea." I shake my head and put the phone down on my lap. "Sorry, but I can't do that. Not with that asshole there. You'll just have to come over here and see her, mom."

My mother's face drops into a look of disappointment and I feel my fucking heart rip apart. I hate seeing her sad.

This woman raised me and is everything good in me. She helped make me who I am today and kept me sane growing up, when I thought all hope was lost. We protected and took care of each other. I can never hurt her.

Well shit . . .

Swallowing, I reach for my phone and stare at it in silence for a few moments, before typing out a message.

> *Styx: Come to dinner with me tomorrow night to meet my mother. You're the first woman I've invited to dinner.*

Looking pleased, my mother stands up and kisses me on the top of the head. "I have a lot of preparing to do. Dinner has to be perfect! These will be the best tacos of your damn life."

"Where are you going?" I ask as she starts walking down the porch steps. "You just got here."

"Out to lunch with Dana and then shopping for a nice outfit. It's been a while and I miss her and your uncle Wes." She winks. "I have to look good for the first woman that my son has invited to dinner. Love you, baby. Don't be late."

I find myself smiling from her excitement and standing up to watch her leave. "Love you too."

Once I'm alone, I jump in the shower and begin thinking about all the bad shit that can happen at a dinner with my father.

I hate the idea of her meeting him, but my mother deserves more from me. Like she says, he's been good for months now, so I can only hope that I won't have a reason to kill him tomorrow.

If he acts up, then Meadow will see a side of me that I'm hoping to never have to show her.

When I'm drying off, my phone vibrates with a message from Meadow. So I drop my towel and reach for it, anxious to see what she has to say.

> *Meadow: I definitely feel special then. I'd be happy to tell your mother stories of your stalkerish behavior Count me in.*

> *Styx: My mother would be proud that I've finally decided to*

find a beautiful as hell woman to stalk and spend more than one night with.

Meadow: Then she'll love my stories and how I much I love that you want to spend more than one night with me.

Her text has me thinking, and before I know it, I'm walking around my house in the nude, thinking about how much of an ass I am for not making more time to learn things about her when we're together.

How the hell am I supposed to give her a good date, when I don't know the first thing about what she likes. I'd like to pretend that I do, but I don't.

Styx: It's occurred to me that I need to learn a lot about you. Hell, I don't even know your favorite damn color. So I'm going to need you to fill out this quick questionnaire.

Styx: Question #1.

Boyshorts? Bikini? Or thong?

Styx: Actually, scratch that. I already know the answer and it's hot as fuck.

Styx: Question #1, take 2.

Does size matter? 'Cause if it does, then I'm good. But does it?

Meadow: LOL. Oh no. I don't know what's going on here or if I should be scared, BUT . . . Yes.

Styx: Question #2.

But yes, what? That I'm good? I thought I pointed out that I already knew this.

I smirk as I type out my next question.

Styx: Question #3.

How many times a night do you fantasize about me? Be honest. Even if it is 10 times or more.

Meadow: Oh you're definitely good. And I'm going to go with at least twelve. And they're extremely HOT. Next question.

Styx: Question #4.

What's your favorite color?

Meadow: Turquoise. Did you toss this in there to throw me off?

I stop in front of my dresser and grab some clothes to throw on, unable to hold back the grin. Fuck, I love having fun with her like this.

Styx: Question #5.

A night on the town or relaxing on the couch with a movie? I can only be naked for one. Keep that in mind.

Meadow: Then definitely relaxing on the couch with a movie and then a night out under the stars with YOU. Any woman would be stupid to say otherwise.

Styx: Okay, for real now. Forget about my smartass comments. What do you truly love to do? I want to know.

Meadow: Please tell me we're not going to go out and sit across the table from each other at a stiff ass restaurant and play 21 questions. What I love is spending time with you and not needing to talk, Styx.

Meadow: I love that all we need when we're together is to just be close. You're my relaxation and what I look forward to after a long day or week at work. I don't feel like words are needed when we're together.

"Holy shit. How did I get so lucky?"

I pull my jeans up and button them, while reading over her messages for a second time.

She knows just the right words to make me want her even more than I already do and suddenly I'm in an even bigger hurry than before to get to her.

Styx: Fuck. Will you marry me?

I'm not really asking of course, but damn, she's definitely wife material. I don't even know how a fucker like me got so damn lucky.

Meadow: Question #6.

I think you forgot that part ;)

Styx: Be ready for me in an hour. I'm coming for you.

Meadow: Oh . . . I'm always ready for you. See you soon.

My front door swings open loud and hard and then I hear the sound of Kash's annoying voice coming from the other room.

"Come on, dick. Let's get some food and beers before my shift. My ass is starving."

Grunting, I walk out to meet Kash by the couch, where he's

now chillin' and watching TV.

"Can't. I'm making dinner for Meadow tonight." Walking to the fridge, I grab two beers and pop the tops. "But I'll have a couple beers so I can handle your presence before I kick you out."

He snatches the beer from me, when I hold it over the couch for him. "No shit." He takes a swig and watches me as I walk around to take a seat on the chair. "It's that serious, huh?"

Smirking, I watch his worried face as he downs half of the beer. "Calm your dick, man. And stop worrying about the damn club and losing business. Cale can find someone else."

"Don't fuck with me, Styx." He looks worried as he stands up and paces in front of me. "Don't tell me you're thinking about leaving WOS. I know that damn look and I don't like it."

I run my hands through my hair, but don't say anything. Kash might just take it harder than Cale will.

"Fuck, man!" I watch as he tosses his beer into the trash and then slams the lid closed. "We started this journey together. You not being there just sounds too damn strange for me to be able to accept that right now."

I stand up and walk over to pour the rest of my beer into the sink. "I'm not saying for sure that I want to leave, but I've been thinking about it for a while now."

"Because of Meadow?" he questions.

"Nah." I shake my head and grip the counter. "I had my fun in the beginning, but it's all just old to me now. I have a gym to run and focus on. It's time for my ass to grow up. I've been considering this before Meadow came into the picture so don't hate on her for it."

"I'm not, but shit." He grabs another beer out and drinks it in silence. "My annoying ass roommate might just squeeze his way into the club after all. He's been on Cale's ass for weeks about getting in."

"Like I said. The club will be fine if I leave. So cheer the fuck up and get out of my house. I have important shit to do and looking at your face isn't on my list."

Kash laughs and finishes off his beer. "Then you need a new list."

He get's ready to walk away, but I stop him, before he reaches the door. "Hey. Don't bring this up to Cale until I think about it some more, alright. I'll talk to him when I'm ready."

"Yeah, I got it," he grumbles. "I better go teach Colt's ass some moves. He can't dance for shit and I'm not having him embarrass me and ruin my good reputation at the club."

"Actually, I need you to grab Stone, Kage and the other two fuckers of WOS and do me a favor first. Don't complain either, because I do a lot of stupid shit when you guys need it. You dicks owe me."

"Shit. What?"

I throw a wad of money his way and grin. "I need a gazebo set up in the back yard in the next forty-five minutes. The couch and the TV need be in it in and set up for movies . Got it?"

I can't help but to smile as I watch him bitch his way out the door. I love the guy, but watching him sweat over shit always seems to put me in a better mood.

Probably because he's been a pain in my ass since the beginning. Just about as much of a pain as Stone's cocky ass.

I spend the thirty minutes preparing dinner, before I rush out to my motorcycle and head toward Meadow's.

Fuck. I hope this night turns out right. This has got to be the most romantic shit I've ever done . . .

chapter EIGHTEEN

STYX

MEADOW LOOKS EXTREMELY SEXY IN the *Victoria's Secret* sweats and tank top that she's wearing and I'm happy that she decided to go with the comfortable look. I'm not really into the whole fancy restaurant bullshit and I'm glad she isn't either.

My eyes wander over her body as she walks ahead of me, going straight for the front door. I'm trying to be respectful, but truthfully, I want to undress her with my damn teeth and skip the dinner.

I'll be her dessert. She can have me anyway she wants me.

She laces her arm around my neck and smiles against my lips, when I stop her from walking into the house. "I smell something delicious. So the sexy alpha cooks." She laughs when I smile against her lips and nod. I'm not gonna lie, I'm proud of my cooking abilities. "I love a man that knows how to cook. It's so damn sexy. A huge turn on."

I grip her hips and brush my lips over hers, trying my best to not just take her right here on the porch. But with her back against the door and my erection pressed against her stomach, it's hard not to think of the possibilities right now. "Then get ready to fall in love. I'm a great fucking cook."

"Is that right?" I bite her bottom lip and she moans into my mouth, while running her hand down the front of my body as if admiring me. "If you're as good at cooking as you are at everything else that you do . . . then I believe it."

She pushes my chest with her finger and then rushes to open the front door, before I can open it for her.

I walk in after her, smiling as she tilts her head back and sniffs the air with a moan. It's so damn sexy. "Holy shit, Styx. It smells even better from inside. I've never had a man cook me dinner before. This is new and I love that you did this."

"I'll do a lot for you," I say, while guiding her to the kitchen table and pulling out a chair for her to sit. Surprisingly she didn't even notice that my couch and TV are gone. She's too focused on dinner. That's what I wanted. "I'm not going to lie. You're the first woman I've cooked for. You're becoming the first for a lot of things for me and it surprises the hell out of me. *You* surprise the hell out of me."

She looks up at me, speechless, before she bites her lip and turns away as if she doesn't want me to see her reaction. Too late. Hiding her face does nothing. Especially with the way she's shifting in her seat and breathing so hard that I can hear it.

My confession made her nervous.

She's falling for me just as hard as I'm beginning to fall for her and I have a feeling that it surprises her just as much.

I stuck the steak and homemade mashed potatoes in the oven, before I left to pick her up. So I pull them out and fix our plates in silence, giving her a moment to gather her thoughts.

The look on her face as I set the table for her is one of admiration and appreciation. It makes my heart speed up to see her looking at me this way. "Thank you," she says sincerely. "I want you to know that I appreciate the things you do for me. It's been a while since I've had anyone be there for me like you have just within the month that I've met you. So thank you."

My heart sinks from the sadness laced in her voice and it brings me back to the conversation we had on the rock about losing her parents when she was young and then her aunt a year ago.

Fuck, I hate the thought of her ever being alone.

It makes me want to be there for her more, but I know it's impossible right now. Not with our busy schedules. But I hope to change that soon.

I sit back and watch as she gets lost in her first few bites of steak. The way her eyes close and that sexy little moan leaves her mouth, tells me that she loves it just as much as I was hoping she would.

"Oh. My. God." When she's done chewing, she opens her eyes and smiles across the table at me. "This is *the* best steak I have ever eaten. No joke. This is insanely good."

"I'm glad to hear that." I cut a piece of my steak and lift a brow, watching as she shoves a huge chunk of hers in her mouth as if she's enjoying it a little too much. "I enjoy how much you love my meat in your mouth."

She stops chewing and throws a green bean at me, trying to hold back her laughter as it bounces off my forehead.

"I didn't mean to hit you in the face, but I have to admit that it is kind of funny." Another green bean hits my forehead, making her laugh even louder.

She's so damn beautiful when she laughs as if no one's watching. Well . . . I definitely am.

With my eyes locked on hers, I pull her chair beside mine and lock it in place with my leg just as I did that night at the club. She continues to laugh at me as I wipe my forehead off and shake my head at her.

"You're lucky you're so damn cute when you laugh." I lick my bottom lip, before leaning in and kissing her, right as she gets ready to speak.

Whatever she was about to say will just have to wait. My mouth needs to be all over hers right now. I can't handle not touching her.

"Oh yeah?" she questions against my lips, before tugging my bottom one with her teeth. "And you're lucky that you're the only thing I've wanted all day. Or else I'd hurt you for keeping me away from this steak."

"Yeah?" I growl, while wrapping my hands into the back of her hair and pulling her closer. "I like a dangerous woman. Go ahead. Hurt me."

She looks at me for a few seconds, her eyes soft, before she speaks. "Honestly, I don't think I could ever hurt you. Even if you wanted me to."

"Good," I whisper. "Now finish your dinner. I have something else planned for us."

I haven't been out back yet, but I hope like hell that the boys came through for me. She wants a night at home, curled up on the couch with movies and then a night out under the stars. With me, she's getting both at the same time.

By the time we're done with dinner, Meadow is looking at me with the biggest smile. She hasn't stopped smiling since we sat down to eat and that makes me happier than anything.

This night is supposed to be all about her and I'm happy that she's excited to see what comes next.

"Best dinner of my life. I'm seriously stuffed. I should've stopped eating a long time ago, but I couldn't. This . . . this was so good. Who taught you how to cook like that?"

I answer her while cleaning up our dirty plates and tossing them into the dishwasher. "My uncle Wes. He's the best cook that I know. So I'll make sure to keep you away from him. I don't need any competition. The fucker's handsome too."

I hear her laugh behind me, before I feel her arms wrap around my waist. "There's never any competition when it comes to you. So I wouldn't worry too much about uncle Wes."

Turning around to face her, I cup her face and lean down to kiss her with a soft moan. "I'm trying really fucking hard to be somewhat romantic so let's get you outside before I blow it and rip your clothes off right here with my damn teeth."

She stands on her tippy toes and wraps her arms around my neck, pulling me down to her with force. "Keep talking to me like that and we might not make it outside for the next part of the date."

With that, she turns and walks away, leaving me to watch her sexy ass as she heads for the back door, stopping once she reaches for the handle. "Come."

Her one-word command has me following her and kissing the back of her neck as she pulls the door open and looks around.

"Styx," she says excitedly, while shoving the screen door open. "What is this?" She walks outside to get a closer look. "Is that your couch and TV?"

"You wanted a night with movies and stars. So you're getting a night with movies and stars. You ask for something with me and I give it. That's how I work."

Grabbing my hand, she starts pulling me toward the gazebo, in a hurry to get me over to the couch. "Wow!" She looks up at the screen roof, her mouth dropping as she looks at all the stars. They're so bright tonight. "I love this! I would've never thought to do anything like this. This is amazing. You never cease to amaze me."

Taking a seat, I pull her down into my lap and wrap my arms around her, just as I did on the rock that night.

Having her in my arms feels so damn good and all I can think about is wanting to protect her and make her happy.

I let her control the remote, until she finds a movie that she wants to watch. The movie doesn't matter to me. It's being here with her in my arms that I've been looking forward to all day and night.

About twenty minutes into the movie, we move positions so that I'm laying behind her, with my arms wrapped tightly around her. I want her as comfortable as she can be.

Even if she falls asleep in my arms. I won't be moving. I'll sleep out here to make her happy.

"Thank you," she whispers half-way through the movie. "This is one of the best nights of my life."

"Good," I whisper back. "It's one of mine too."

She flips around to face me, wrapping her arms around my head. "You're so much different than I expected, Styx. Sweeter and more caring. One of the most caring people I've ever met. You make me feel . . . just . . . you make me feel. It's been a long time since I've cared about anything other than the hospital."

I feel an ache in my chest as I hold her as tightly as I can and place my forehead to hers. "You make me feel too. You're the first woman to make me want more in life. The first woman that I've spent my days looking forward to seeing any chance that I can get. You're special to me."

Her breathing picks up against my lips. "I go to sleep at night thinking about being with you. I miss you when you're not around. That's a big deal for me."

Leaning up, I cup her face and crush my lips against hers, wanting nothing more than to feel her against me.

This woman is everything I've been looking for and holy

fuck . . . hearing that she misses me when I'm not around has me going fucking crazy inside.

Gently, I flip her around to her back and press my body in between her legs. "What do you miss about me?" I ask in a whisper.

"The way you make me laugh and forget about the emptiness that I've felt since losing my aunt. The way you kiss me as if you can't get enough of me. And the way you hold me in silence as if words aren't needed to describe what you're feeling for me."

Our hearts race against each other's as I trace her bottom lip with my thumb and hover my mouth above hers. "Fuck, I want you as mine."

"Then take me," she breathes. "I can be yours if you want me to."

Sitting up, I pull my shirt over my head and toss it down. Her hands slowly roam over my body, caressing my muscles as I reach for my jeans and undo them.

Her touch is gentle and caring as if she's taking the time to remember this moment forever. Like she's burning it into her brain for later.

I am too.

My heart is racing so fast and hard that I know she must feel it as I pull her up and strip her of her shirt and bra.

"You're so beautiful."

Before I know it, our naked bodies are tangled together and I'm slowly sinking into her under the stars.

Our bodies move slowly this time. Gentle as my bare cock fills her, causing her to moan into my mouth and scratch my back as if she's more lost in the moment than any other time we've had sex.

It may be gentler, but there's nothing gentle about the emotions that this is bringing out of her. Hell, out of the both of us.

"Oh fuck . . ." I moan out as I move inside of her, feeling her bare. It's almost too much to handle. "You're so wet for me, baby. I love feeling you this way."

Her fingers dig into my back and her legs squeeze my ass as I push in as deep as I can go and stop. "Me too," she breathes. "Oh my God you feel so good. Keep moving for me."

This must be what making love feels like. Holy fuck. It's better than any rough night of sex that I've ever had.

I'll take this every damn night if I can have it with her.

I feel myself getting close to release, so I wrap my hands into her hair and whisper against her lips. "Can I come in you?"

She nods and then kisses me so hard and deep that I know she wants me to just as badly as I want to.

I pull her up so that she's straddling my lap, my hands tugging at her hair as she rides me slow and deep, until I'm filling her with my come.

A few seconds later, her grip on me tightens as she clenches around my cock, moaning against my mouth as her whole body shakes with pleasure.

"Holy shit, Styx." She breathes. "I honestly didn't think that sex with you could get any better . . . but it just did. You're amazing."

I kiss her and hold her against me, feeling our hearts beat together.

After we have both caught our breath, I clean us up and then pull the blanket from the back of the couch, covering us up with her in my arms.

Holy shit. I think I'm screwed after this. There's no way I'm letting another man ever be inside her this way . . .

chapter NINETEEN

Meadow

AFTER STYX SHOWED ME AN incredibly amazing night, I fell asleep in his arms, laying under the stars in the gazebo.

It was peaceful and beautiful. Nothing else mattered in that moment except my heart beating against his as he held me to his chest, making it seem that he couldn't get me close enough.

Going home this morning sucked and truthfully made me wish that we had the whole day free to just lounge around and hold each other.

But he had to go to the gym for most of the afternoon so he dropped me off at home, leaving my whole body aching for his touch, impatient to see him again tonight.

I've spent most of my morning now, trying to talk one of the other nurses into covering my shift so that I can make it to his mother's dinner tonight to repay him for everything he's done for me.

After two hours on the damn phone and promising Dani that I'll work a double tomorrow, I'm finally free today.

And I've spent every last second since hanging up that phone reliving last night and trying to figure out what is happening between Styx and I.

A month ago if you would've asked me if I was ready for a serious relationship, I would've said no. I was scared. Terrified of getting used to being with someone and loving them just to possibly end up alone *again*. I've lost too much and the pain is still unbearable at times.

I'm still afraid, but truthfully all I want to do is spend my time with Styx.

I get that Styx doesn't open up much to others. I get that he's not typically the romantic, serious relationship type guy, but he makes me feel that for me- he would be. And I love that. It gives me hope that things could be more than I expected.

Mandy has been watching me try on outfits for the last hour now, but I can't seem to find one that I'm completely satisfied with. What a way to spend her night off.

"The last three outfits looked good. What are you so worried about?" she asks as she watches from her seat on my bed. "He invited you home to meet his mother. From what I've heard about this guy, I doubt he cares what you're wearing. He'll just be happy to have you there."

"Yeah." I turn away from the mirror to face her. "I know. But just knowing that I'm the first woman he's invited to dinner with his mother . . . You get it. I just want to look nice. For her."

Mandy smiles at me. "I've never seen you like this over a man before, Meadow. It makes me happy because you deserve to feel this. You deserve someone who will give to you as much as you do to others. You're a good person."

She stands up and fixes the back of my black blouse. "I know you've lost a lot. But *please* try not to let that discourage you from getting close with Styx. I know it has in the past. But honestly . . . none of those men seemed to be worth it. Especially not Jase."

A tear falls from my eye and I laugh, wiping it away. No one has really mentioned that they think I give a lot. Not since my aunt has passed at least. She used to remind me that all the time when it came to guys.

"*Especially* not that ass. He was never more than just something to pass the time and I was the same to him."

"Are you sure about that?" she asks as I'm throwing my hair up.

"Why do you ask that? Of course that's all he was for me."

"I meant for him. He's been acting strange ever since you and Styx started dating. He's been very moody and almost lost in his own little world most of the time. It's weird. He hasn't even been sleeping around with the other nurses. Weird. I hate *this* Jase even more."

I sit down on the edge of my bed and slip my black heeled boots on, tucking the legs of my skinny jeans inside. "Doesn't matter. Jase is in the past. So let's not talk about him anymore. Especially when I'm about to see Styx. He'll be here any minute."

She reaches for her purse and walks past the mirror, giving herself a quick glance. "Tell me all about dinner later, okay. I want to know how it goes. Jameson is waiting for me so I should go."

Smiling, I give her a quick hug and then walk her to the door. "Have fun on your date, babe. And don't think that I won't be asking for details later. Details for details. Sounds like a fair exchange."

"You got it." She winks and jogs down the porch steps as Styx pulls up on his motorcycle. "Holy hell . . . he's hot on a motorcycle." Giving me the thumbs up, she turns away and walks past Styx, waving before she jumps into her car.

"Hell yeah he is," I whisper to myself, while looking him over on his bike.

I swear a man has never made a leather jacket look so damn good. It's my favorite thing of his that he wears.

After I quickly lock my door, I turn around and watch as he pulls his helmet off and walks toward me.

Even his walk is extremely sexy and full of confidence and the thought that this guy was inside of me without a condom last night has me fanning myself off with my purse.

I think I'm going to overheat. Especially if he keeps looking at me with those sexy blue eyes the way that he is.

As if he's about to tie me up and devour me.

"Come here," he says, while pulling me against him. "Holy fuck, I've missed you all day."

His hands grip the back of my hair and before I know it, his lips crash against mine, taking my damn breath away.

The way his tongue moves against mine, his soft lips all over my lips as if he owns them. This kiss is different than the rest. Deeper and more meaningful somehow.

Or maybe it's just my imagination.

He pulls away from our kiss, placing his forehead against mine. "You ready to meet my mother?"

I can tell from the look in his eyes that he's worried about bringing me to his mother's house. I'm not sure what to think about that. Maybe I was right to worry about what to wear.

"Are you sure you want me to go? I don't have to . . ."

He kisses me again, but harder this time, backing me up against the door and pinning me in with his body. "Fuck yes I do. Don't ever question that again. It's not you."

I look up to meet his gaze. "Tell me why you're nervous."

His eyes close and he lets out a deep breath, speaking with our foreheads still pressed together. "My asshole father will be there and there's a lot of things that you don't know about him. He's hurt both me and my mother a lot."

I reach up and cup his face, my heart breaking as I look into his eyes. "I'm sorry that he's ever hurt you or your mother. I hate hearing that with everything in me. I know you said he was an asshole . . ."

"He's a piece of shit. The biggest asshole that I know and honestly he doesn't even deserve to be in the same room with you, but I'm doing this for my mother."

Standing up on my tippy toes, I press my lips to his, talking against them. "He doesn't deserve a son like you. You're so far from being an asshole. You're the best person I know. So let's just go and prove to him that you're the bigger person. Let's not worry. Okay? I'm here for you."

He nods his head and breathes against my lips. "And I love you for that."

"Fuck," he whispers afterwards and turns away in a hurry, grabbing my hand to walk me down to his bike. "Let's go."

I try to focus on jumping on the back of his motorcycle and wrapping my arms around him, but all my mind is on is the fact that the word *love* just came from his lips. Even if it wasn't in the *I love you* way.

It has my heart racing and my whole body feeling weak.

This man has much more of me than I thought. He has my fucking heart. All of it and I hope like hell that he doesn't rip it from my chest.

When we pull up at his parents' house, his whole body stiffens as he stares at the empty driveway.

"Everything alright?" I ask in his ear. "Is anyone here?"

He turns off the engine, but doesn't make a move to get off his bike. "Yeah, my mother's here. My father isn't."

I smile and rub his shoulders. "That's a good thing then,

right? Maybe he'll miss dinner and you won't have to-"

"It's not a good thing," he growls, while helping me off the back of his bike. "Trust me. It's far from good."

Grabbing my hand, he gives me a quick kiss on the lips, before walking me to the house and pushing the door open.

"We're here, mom."

A beautiful woman about my height comes running from the kitchen, excitedly pulling her blonde hair from her face and pinning it back. "Oh. My."

She stops in front of me and looks me over, before pulling my hand from Styx's and enclosing it in hers. "Meadow is *beautiful*." I laugh nervously as she spins me around and then hugs me. "You're perfect for my son. Just think of the beautiful babies ya'll would have."

"Seriously?" Styx says, sounding embarrassed. "Let's not talk about kids when she's barely been mine for a month. Shit, mom."

"So she is yours?" she questions, looking as if she got the information a lot easier than she expected. Grinning, she throws her arms around me and whispers, "You're the first woman he's *ever* called his. You're special to him and that makes you very special to me."

"Alright. Alright. Try not to scare Meadow away before she even makes it to the kitchen table to fucking eat. Now where's Frank?"

His mom smiles even bigger and then kisses him on the forehead. "Love you, baby," she says, ignoring his question. "Now let's go eat."

Styx grabs my hand as his mom rushes back into the kitchen as if to avoid any further talk of his father. "My mother's a little excited about tonight. So ignore some of the things she says.

She's not used to me bringing women around."

I smile and squeeze his hand, excited to get to experience this. "I love her. She's so cute. I love that she's excited so let's try to forget about your father and enjoy this time with her. I want her to be happy. I want to see you both smiling tonight."

I give him a quick kiss and then head to the kitchen to help his mother.

Styx follows shortly behind, going straight to the dishes to help set the table.

"Meadow, sweetie." His mother turns to look at me, while shoving a piece of hamburger meat in her mouth. "Would you mind grabbing the cheese from the bottom drawer in the fridge? I forgot to get it out. Everything is set after that!"

"No problem," I say, returning her smile. "Thanks for having me for dinner. It smells delicious in here."

She laughs. "I learned from my son. I was a lousy cook when he was a kid and none of my food had any flavor."

I catch Styx laughing as he finishes setting up the table. "That's true. I used to go weeks skipping dinner just so I wouldn't have to eat her cooking."

"Hey!" His mother throws a taco shell at him. "That's a lie. You make it sound as if I fed you dog food as a kid." She winks. "It was cat food."

I can't help but to laugh as we all sit down and start making our tacos.

I can definitely see where Styx gets his personality from.

After dinner, we spend the next hour at the table eating snacks and playing cards, listening to stories about when Styx was a teen.

A smile hasn't left our faces since we sat down and I have to admit that this is the best family dinner I've had since I was a kid.

I've forgotten what it was like to have a family. I'm glad that Styx has one and that he has the choice to still experience these moments.

There's just one thing that's been bothering me.

Every few minutes, I catch Styx looking toward the living room with a worried expression as if he's waiting for his father to show up at any minute.

I just wish I knew a way to take his worry away. But I don't and I hate it . . .

STYX

I'M TRYING MY BEST TO enjoy the night with the two most important people in my life, but I can't stop thinking about that asshole and when he's going to show up and ruin everything.

He's going to be here any damn second. I can feel it in my fucking bones and I will do everything in my power to protect the both of them. Nothing about this night is going to end well and I'm already hating that I've put Meadow in this position.

I stare hard. Waiting . . .

Come on, motherfucker and get it over with.

"Styx!" My mother laughs and tosses a card at me to get my attention. It's about the fifth time that she's had to yell at me since the game started. I'm trying hard to just be in the moment, but I can't. Fuck, it's hard to concentrate right now. "It's your turn again. Go! Don't keep us ladies waiting all night. That's rude."

"Sorry. I was just . . ." I pull my eyes away from the living room and get ready to toss a card down to play, when the front door bursts open, causing everyone at the table to jump in surprise. Myself included and I fucking hate my body for reacting this way.

I spent my whole childhood fearing this man, but not anymore. He will never get the pleasure of seeing fear in my eyes again. I will die before that day happens.

"Oh fuck," my mom whispers, while panicking to push all of the cards into a pile.

Meadow must see the worry on her face, so she jumps to her feet and starts gathering cards too, without question. "Let me help you." She places her hands on my mother's as she continues to reach out with shaky hands. "I got it. It's okay."

Jumping to my feet, I stand straight, cracking my neck as I watch the drunken bastard enter the kitchen and stop.

Yeah, you want to stand there looking like an ass as if you didn't know we would be here. You want to play this shit so you have an excuse to be angry.

Keeping my eyes on him, I watch as he tilts back the rest of what's left of his beer and then tosses the empty bottle in the sink.

"What the fuck is this shit, Lily?" He grips the sink, before punching the counter and then turning around to face us. "You didn't tell me we'd have guests. I would've made sure to come home right after work."

My mother looks from Meadow to me and shakes her head apologetically. "I told you yesterday, remember? I mentioned going to buy stuff for tacos . . ."

"The fuck you did," he shouts, while picking up the closest thing to him and throwing it across the room. His jaw clenches as his eyes land on the cards that Meadow is shoving into the box. "You fucking play cards without me, Lily? Get over here. Now."

"Fuck you," I growl out, while blocking my mother from

his view. He won't live to hurt her again if he makes any move to touch her. "She doesn't have to come to you. Don't ever fucking talk to her like that again. You need to leave."

"I need to leave?" He points at his chest and laughs his asshole fucking laugh that he always does. As if he's so damn untouchable. Not anymore. "This is *my* house. *I* pay the bills. No one tells me what to do in my own home. Not even your bitch of a mother."

"Woah! Don't talk like that about her. What is your problem?" Meadow speaks up, causing my father to look at her for what must be the first time since he's walked in the door.

I instantly stiffen up at even the idea of his eyes on her. They're dark and full of whatever evil resides inside his fucked up mind.

"Who the fuck is this little bitch in my house?" His hand slips from the counter, him nearly falling down, but he somehow manages to catch himself first. "Dammit, Lily. I'm going to beat your ass for making me look like a fool. Come. Here. Now."

In a rage, he pushes me to the side to get at my mother, but I grab him by his neck, slamming him into the sink. "You will *never* talk to my mother or girlfriend with that disrespect again. I will cut your fucking tongue from your mouth. Got it?" I look over my shoulder at Meadow, while preventing my father from moving. "I need you both outside. Now. Take my mom. Don't let her back in no matter what she says."

Meadow nods her head and shoots to her feet.

"Don't you dare fucking go outside, Lily. You will stay right there until I say so. This asshole won't touch me with you around to see it and as soon as he gets the fuck out of the way, you're mine. Stay," he demands.

Feeling the rage take over, I toss him down onto the kitchen floor and grab him by the throat, squeezing so hard that he starts

coughing. "Let's see you try to touch her now, you piece of shit."
I elbow him in the face as he attempts to push me away. "Go
ahead. Hurt her! Do it motherfucker. Get past me now. Let me
see you try. Put your hands on her like you have since I was ten.
Make her scream and cry, balled up on the floor trying to protect
herself. Go ahead!"

"Fuck you and that bitch of a mother of yours," he chokes
out. "She's not good for anything but a quick fuck anyway and
she won't even give that any-"

I see red and my fist connects with his face, cutting him off
before he can finish his thoughts.

I will not sit here and listen to him disrespect my mother
anymore.

Feeling the fire inside me build up, I lose all restraint, my
fists continuing to swing over and over again.

The only sound filling my ears is my fist connecting hard
with his bones. Again. Again. And again until his face is covered
in blood and I feel hands pull at me, trying to get me off of him.

It takes a few seconds for me to come back to the scene
around me enough to realize that my mother is crying and
screaming at me to stop, while Meadow is telling me he's had
enough.

They both sound worried and that's when I notice that my
father isn't moving anymore or struggling to get away from me.

Releasing his throat, I fight to catch my breath while looking hard to see that he's knocked out cold. He's done for. He's
had enough- she's right.

Although in my mind, it can never be enough.

Blood covers his face and my hands, but I don't feel one
ounce of regret seeing him lay there helpless in his own pool of
blood. I've seen my mother do the same too many times.

"What did you do?" my mom cries. "You could've killed

him." She pushes at me, screaming and crying. "He wasn't going to touch me. He wasn't." She pushes me again and then drops down to her knees.

I stand up and watch as my mother grabs at his shirt and yells his name in attempt to get him to wake up.

"Frank! Get up! Open your eyes." She slaps his cheek in a panic. "Come on, dammit! Open them."

This only pisses me off more, watching her in so much agony over his pain. He deserved every hit that he took. "After everything he's put you through. Us through. You give a shit about *him* being hurt for once? After all those times he hurt you every fucking day and then beat me for trying to help you? All the broken bones I suffered as a child because of him or all of the scars on the back of your head from him throwing you into anything and everything."

I grip at my hair and start pacing. I want to fucking scream, but I'm trying my best not to scare Meadow anymore or give her a reason to think I'm anything like that piece of shit on the floor. "Why the fuck haven't you left him yet? Why the fuck did you put us through all that suffering after seeing how dangerous he *was*. He could've killed us both. But you stayed anyway and you still refuse to leave. Why the hell won't you walk away? Why? Tell me."

"Stop it, Styx. Dammit. Stop it," she cries out, while wiping at her face. "I love him and he hasn't hurt me in over six months. Things have been good between us and you just ruined that. He's going to hate me now." She cries harder and I can tell that it's out of fear.

I haven't forgotten that sound. I'll never forget that fucking sound.

"He hasn't hurt you in six months," I scream. "You want to know why? It's because of me. Fuck!" I point at my chest in pain.

"Because I sit outside your house every fucking day when he gets off work, making sure that he can walk straight. Making sure that he hasn't been drinking so he won't feel the need to beat you for no reason. That's why he hasn't hurt you. I make sure of it. He knows I'm there every single fucking day. That's why."

I glance over at Meadow to see her watching us with her hand over her mouth and tears spilling from her eyes. She's pained by everything that she's learning about our past and it only makes me love her more.

Fuck, I hate that she has to see this, but there's no stopping this shit storm now. There's no walking away from this situation.

This is my mother and my father. This is my life. It's been my shitty life since the day my father picked up a beer and never put one down.

My mother looks up from trying to get my father to respond to her. "You do that for me?" she questions with tears in her eyes. "Every day?"

I nod my head and reach for my mother's hand to pull her up to her feet. "Damn straight I do. I'd do anything for you. I'd fucking die for you. No questions asked."

My mom's arms wrap around my neck and before I know it, she's bawling into my arms, me holding her up so she won't fall to the floor. "I'm so sorry. I'm so damn sorry. Oh my God." She holds me tighter, her whole body shaking as she cries. "I'm hurting you. It's me. I've been the one hurting you."

I glance over to see more tears roll down Meadow's face, before she wipes them away and walks over to check my father's pulse and breathing.

It hurts me so damn much right now that she has to be here to witness this shitty mess and check to make sure that I haven't just killed someone right in front of her eyes.

Fuck, she may hate me after this.

Once my mom calms down, I release my hold on her and walk over to throw my arms around Meadow when she steps away from Frank. "I'm so fucking sorry. I promise you that this isn't me. This pain has been building for years and I can't stand back anymore while that piece of shit hurts my mother." I kiss her cheek and whisper in her ear. "You can leave if you want. I'll understand."

She shakes her head and then cups my face, pulling me in for a kiss. She's soft and gentle, her lips still wet from the tears she's shed. "I could never leave you for having a heart and wanting to protect your family. *No one* deserves to hurt like this. I would've done it my damn self."

She pulls away and looks me in the eyes when the drunken bastard makes noises as if he's about to vomit and mumbles my mother's name. "I hate to say this, but your dad can't be left alone tonight. He could asphyxiate on his own vomit. He's drunk and covered in his own blood."

I see my mother looking down at that piece of shit as if she wants to help him and lessen his suffering. "I'll stay with him. Help me roll him over to his side." She looks up at me, waiting.

Rushing to her, I pull my mom away from the piece of shit and roll him over with force, just in time for him to throw up on the carpet.

"There's no way in hell I'm letting you stay here with him so he can beat the shit out of you when he gets back to his feet. No fucking way, mom. Not happening."

I see the panic in my mother's eyes and I hate seeing her this way. It has my heart feeling like it's being ripped in two. I hate that asshole, but I love her more.

"As a nurse I can't just leave him here with the possibility of him dying, Styx. I hate what he's done just as much as you do, but someone needs to be here. I'll stay for a few hours if I have to."

"Fuck no." Frustrated, I run my hands through my hair and then grab Meadow's hand, walking her over to my mother. "I'll stay with the piece of shit so he doesn't die. You guys take the car and stay at my place."

"Styx?" Meadow questions. "Are you sure you can handle this?"

I shake my head. "No . . . but I'll do it for you two." I kiss the top of my mother's head and then wrap my arms around Meadow, giving her a gentle kiss. "You two take of each other until I can, please. That's all I ask. You can leave after that if you want, but please take care of each other for tonight."

I look into my mother's exhausted eyes. They're red and puffy from crying and she looks as if she's about to fall over. "Please go with Meadow for tonight. I need you out of here. I need to know that you're safe. If anything, do it for me. Fall asleep knowing that this asshole won't hurt you for once. One fucking night that you won't have to worry. I won't let that happen. He's not leaving this house."

She nods her head and wipes at her eyes. "I'm so sorry I ruined the night. I love you so much. I don't want to hurt you anymore. I won't. You're my baby." She grabs my face. "Please. I need help to stay away from him. I can't do it alone."

"You won't have to," I point out. "You're never alone. I'm here."

Meadow jumps in and grabs my mom's hand, before wrapping an arm around her to console her. "I can get you help if you want it, Lily. We can talk about it after you rest."

Walking my mom toward the door, Meadow looks over her shoulder and whispers something that I can't quite understand.

As much as I'd love to ask her what that was, at this point, I'm just happy to see her and my mother walking out that door.

Fuck . . . this is going to be a long night . . .

chapter
TWENTY-ONE

Meadow

IT WAS A ROUGH NIGHT for Lily, but she finally fell asleep just after one this morning once she promised me she'd get herself some help to stay away from Frank.

I spent most of our time together convincing her that she'll be okay without him and that a real man that loved his family wouldn't hurt them. When a real man loves his family, he does everything in his power to protect them.

Like Styx . . .

The son that *she* raised.

She deserves so much more than what Frank's ever given her and I'm just glad that my words made her somewhat see that.

My heart instantly ached for Styx the moment he walked through his door early this morning, looking tired and worn out, but unfortunately I couldn't stay to comfort Styx and let him know that I'm here for him.

Dani reamed my ass over the phone and only gave me fifteen minutes to make it to the hospital. I was already thirty minutes late so I don't blame her.

I practically begged to work a double today so that I could take yesterday off and now I wish with everything in me that I had today off too so I could spend time with Styx and make sure that he's okay.

I've been here for over fifteen hours now and the *only* thing that's been on my mind is Styx. I miss him like crazy.

My heart aches every time I think about him and what he had to do last night. I want to be there for him. I *should* be there for him.

As much as I want to talk to him though, I haven't messaged him because I know he's taking the day off to spend with Lily.

They need this time together and I will never get in the way of them having it. I've never seen a mother than needs her son as much as she needs Styx right now.

I'm off in an hour so if he's free then I'll let him come to me when he's ready.

For now, I'll just do my best to focus on my duties here at the hospital.

As hard as that might be . . .

I'VE BEEN HOME FOR ALMOST an hour, so exhausted that I can barely even stand, but that hasn't stopped my mind from worrying about Styx.

I left my phone in the bedroom when I changed so I didn't even know Styx must've been texting me, until I hear a knock at the door.

Jumping up from the couch, I rush over to open it so fast that I don't even have time to pay attention to who's standing on my porch until it's too late.

Jase pushes past my arm, letting himself inside. "We need to talk, Meadow. I can't handle this shit."

"Jase," I growl. "There's nothing to talk about so I'm going to ask you this nicely. And I will only ask nicely once. Please leave. It's late and I'm exhausted."

Shaking his head, he yanks at his hair and comes at me, grabbing my arms. "I miss you. I didn't think I cared about you as much as I do until I saw you with that asshole."

Not liking his closeness, I yank my arms away from him and start backing away. "Have you been drinking?" I point toward the opened door. "Leave. Right. Now."

He laughs and takes a step toward me, reaching out his arms. "Did you listen to anything I just said? I care about you. I want you."

I keep backing up, until I'm pressed against the wall with Jase blocking me in with his arms. This is the *last* position I want to be in with him. Especially when he's been drinking. I've already watched one drunken asshole make a fool of himself. I don't need to see another one.

"I'm sorry, Jase, but no." I place my hand on his hard chest and give him a shove, but he doesn't budge. "Get the fuck out."

He shakes his head and then grabs my wrist, hard, holding it still so he can lean in and attempt to kiss me.

I turn my head to the side and fight to get my wrist free. "Get the fuck off me, Jase!" I scream and push at him with all my might. "Don't you kiss me. Get off!"

Clenching his jaw, he picks me up and tosses me onto the couch, before throwing himself on top of me and kissing me.

He forces his mouth on mine so hard that I cut my lip on his tooth. Before I know it, his erection is pressed between my legs.

"You used to love this. Remember? Give me a chance to remind you."

"Get off!" I thrust my hips and yell, until I feel his body

weight lift off of me and then hear the sound of bone meeting bone.

Surprised, I sit up, fighting to catch my breath as I watch Styx, beating the shit out of Jase.

Shock takes over and for a second, I can't speak. All I can do is jump over the couch to get away from them.

The punches only seem to get harder and louder with each swing, until Jase finally throws his hands up in surrender.

Breathing hard, Styx shoves Jase's head into the floor, one last time, before jumping to his feet and rushing over to me.

His bloodied hands reach for my face, but I back away, before he can touch me.

"Are you okay? Did he hurt you?"

I close my eyes and run my hands over my face, still shocked as hell that this all just happened.

"I just need him out of here. I can't look at him. I can't." I open my eyes and look at Styx to see his reaction.

Nodding his head, he yanks Jase to his feet and begins pushing him toward the door. "Don't ever fucking come here again," he growls. "You're lucky I didn't kill you for putting your hands on her."

Turning away from Styx, I powerwalk to the bathroom and shut the door behind me, pacing back and forth.

My heart is racing so fast and hard right now that I can hardly catch my breath.

I don't know what to think. I'm so fucking confused. This is all too overwhelming for me.

This all has me wanting to scream. So I do.

Rushing from the bathroom, I grab Styx by the back of his jacket and turn him around, crushing my lips against his, before taking a step back and yelling. "What the fuck!" I look over his shoulder to see Jase opening the door to his car and speeding off.

"You're so much bigger than him. You could've killed him, Styx. You need to know when to stop throwing the punches. Sometimes it doesn't take twenty swings to get the message across."

Styx's eyes soften once he sees how worked up I am. "I wanted to kill him when I walked in that door to see him hurting you. He's lucky he didn't get fifty swings."

God. I love him for this, but feel like I should be mad at the same damn time.

"I understand that you were just protecting me, but I can't handle this right now. Do you understand that in less than twenty-four hours, I stood back and watched you beat the shit out of two grown men? My heart aches seeing you this way."

Pushing his hair out of his face, he walks toward me, not stopping until his body is pressed against mine. "I'm sorry I've made you watch, but I'm not sorry for hurting him. I will do everything to protect you. That's just who I am. Can you handle that?"

Closing my eyes, I nod my head and kiss him back, when I feel his lips on mine.

Being in his arms feels so damn good. Too good, but I think I need to be alone right now.

"I want to be with you tonight, Styx. I do with everything in me, but I need some alone time right now. Is that okay?"

"You want me to leave?" His body stiffens and I hate that a part of him is worried that I might now want him anymore.

"Just for tonight. I just need to draw a hot bath and relax and then go to sleep and wake up to a better day. I think we both need to sleep today off. I know it's been a rough day for you and it's been extremely rough for me too."

He presses his face into my neck, before he gently kisses it and takes a step away from me. "I need to stop by the club to talk to Cale tomorrow. So I guess I need tonight to think about what I want to say to him."

"Is everything okay?" I question.

He nods and zips up his jacket. "Yeah, it will be. Goodnight."

Standing next to the couch, I watch as he walks away and closes the door behind him.

The first thing I do is fall to my knees and cry, letting out all of my frustration and pain.

I feel so damn alone right now, but I need to be.

After spending the whole day at the hospital looking after hurt patients, the last thing that I could take tonight was seeing another person bleeding in front of me, right on my living room floor. I've seen too much blood in the last twenty-four hours. I can't see anymore right now.

Not to mention that I've been thinking about my mother, father and aunt since last night.

But especially my aunt since she raised me for as long as I can remember.

Spending the night with Lily reminded me what it was like to have that warm, fuzzy feeling of a parent being around to talk to.

Sometimes when I'm in moods like this, being alone is the best thing I can do. I hate letting anyone see just how broken I truly am.

I just hope that Styx will understand tomorrow . . .

chapter
TWENTY-TWO

STYX

I HAVEN'T SPOKEN TO MEADOW since last night when she asked me to leave.

I've spent the first part of my day at the gym and the second part of it at my mother's house, making sure that her locks are all properly changed now that Frank has been asked to leave.

The police escorted him out the other night and I made it clear to him that he wasn't to step foot into this house again.

I'll pay the rent for as long as my mother needs. So that piece of shit has no hold over her now. If she needs someone she can call me and I'll be there every single time. She doesn't have to be alone and she won't be.

I'm now on my way to the club to talk to Cale, even though the only thing on my mind is going to find Meadow.

I need to know that she still wants me and that I haven't scared her off. I know she said that she just needed the night, but now that she's had time to think, maybe she needs more. I don't know.

Pulling up to the club, I feel and look like shit as I hop off my motorcycle and make my way inside.

It's not extremely busy here yet, but the instant I get spotted in the crowd, half-naked girls cling to me, pulling me in different directions to get my attention.

It only reminds me more why I need to get the hell out of this place and focus on the gym more.

Having other women's hands on me makes me feel guilty as hell. The only hands that feel good on me are Meadow's.

She's the *only* person I want touching me.

Ignoring the women groping at me, I make my way up the steps to Cale's office and knock.

"It's open."

Cale stands up and walks over to shake my hand once I step inside. "Everything good, man? You look like hell."

I let out a deep laugh and take a seat in the chair across from his. "It's been a rough couple of days, man. Real fucking tough."

"Yeah, I heard." He leans back in his chair and runs a hand through his blonde hair.

I feel like we've all been through a lot together here, watching each other grow and Cale is probably the best fucker I know. Quitting on him is going to be hard.

"Slade tell you?" I question.

He nods his head. "Yeah. But that asshole deserved it. Tell your mother hi for me and if she needs anything to get ahold of Riley or myself. We'll help in any way that we can."

My lips turn up into a thankful smile, but inside I'm feeling guilty as shit. "Appreciate that, man." I run my hands over my face and lean back in the chair, trying to get the words to come out.

"Relax," Cale says. "You might forget that I talk to Slade every damn day. I know what you're here for and I don't want you feeling guilty. It's not like I expect you guys to stay here forever." He laughs when I raise a brow. "Hell, I was happy as hell the day I stopped shaking my dick for money. Trust me. The time will come when Stone and Kash leave too. I'm always prepared. No worries."

"Can't tell Slade anything, apparently," I say with a grin. "That fucker."

Cale shrugs. "He wouldn't have told me if he wasn't trying to look out for you. I know Slade better than anyone else. That just means that he thinks of you as one of our family."

I stand up and shake Cale's hand. "You dicks will always be family to me. Thanks, man. But I got somewhere to be now."

He smiles and starts going through some files. "Looks like I have some auditions to set up. So get out."

I grip the back of the chair and push it to his desk, before hurrying out of his office and through the club, before some random chick can stop me.

There's only one place I want to be right now . . .

Meadow

I'VE HAD THIS ACHE IN my chest all day to see Styx, but I've been fighting it, afraid of what to say to him.

He was there for me when I needed him and I had the nerve to ask him to leave so that I could be alone for the night.

I feel like the biggest asshole and there really aren't any words to explain how sorry I am.

Honestly, I felt even shittier as the night went on. All I wanted to do was curl up in bed, wrapped in his strong arms, but because of me, that didn't happen.

Pulling my truck into Styx's driveway, I sit for a few minutes, while trying to figure out how to explain to him that I have really bad days sometimes and just need to be alone.

I never meant to make him feel the way he felt when walking out my door. I'll never forget the look of hurt on his face when I asked him to leave.

"Okay, you can do this." Shaking off my nerves, I jump out of my truck and walk over to his porch, stopping at the door.

I take a few deep breaths and slowly release them before knocking.

"Please be here," I whisper. "Please."

I feel my heart crush once I realize that he isn't here. I've already driven by the gym on the way here and didn't see his motorcycle. The only other place I can think of him being is the club.

A room full of hot, horny girls screaming and groping at Styx is the last place I want to be at right now.

I honestly don't know if I'd be able to handle that. Not with all of the emotions running through me right now.

Jumping back into my truck, it clicks that he might be at his mother's house. So I drive by to see that all the lights are off and his motorcycle isn't anywhere in sight.

Feeling defeated, I head home, pulling out my phone to text Styx.

I at least want him to know that I'm thinking about him.

Me: I want to see you so bad right now.

A few seconds later, my phone vibrates in my hand with a reply from Styx. My heart races as I open his reply.

Styx: Then get out of that truck and come to me.

Tossing my phone into the passenger seat, I hurry out of my truck to see Styx sitting on my porch, waiting for me.

I can hardly breathe as he starts toward me, dressed in that damn leather jacket of his and ripped up jeans that I love so much.

"Holy shit," I whisper into his arms as he pulls me into him and squeezes. "It feels so good to see you. I'm so sorry. I can explain."

His familiar scent surrounds me as his hands move up to cup my face. "You don't need to explain shit to me. You needed the night to yourself and you asked for it." He presses his forehead to mine, while running his thumb over my lip. The feel of his breath against my face brings me peace. "It feels good to see you too. Honestly, nothing fucking feels better. You have no idea."

He gently sucks my bottom lip into his mouth, before kissing me and whispering," I hated being away from you for the last two nights. Fuck, it made my heart ache so damn bad for you."

My arms wrap around his neck and pull him closer to me, before telling him how I feel. "I barely fell asleep, because all I could think about was being wrapped in your arms and how it feels to fall asleep next to you. I've *never* had a man make me feel so safe and protected before. You're the best thing that's happened to me for as long as I can remember."

His kiss is desperate, almost knocking me off my feet as he spins us around to press me against the door. "Fuck, you have no idea how much that means to me. I want you so damn bad. I've never wanted to call a woman mine so much in my entire life. I want you." He whispers the last part.

His whisper has my heart going crazy for him. This man is everything I want in my life, but am afraid to keep. "Are you sure about that?" I question. "I have a lot of ugly days that I can barely even get out of bed, Styx. I get too lost in my head and need my space from the world." I close my eyes in shame and hide my face in his neck. "I try my best to be strong, but when you've felt alone for as long as I have, after you've lost *everyone* you have ever loved . . . giving yourself to someone else isn't the easiest. I'm so damn scared of being left alone again."

"Fuck," he whispers into the top of my head. "I love you. I'm not going anywhere even if you push me out the damn door. I *never* want you to be afraid with me."

I look up to meet his eyes, my heart pretty much stopping in my chest from his confession. "Did you mean what you just said?" I ask softly.

His grip around me tightens, until there's no space between us. I couldn't get away, even if I wanted to. Which I don't. I never want to get away from this man.

"With everything in me. I've been thinking it for days, but just haven't said it. I was hoping my actions were loud enough to show you. But yes. I fucking love you," he breathes across my lips.

"I love you too," leaves my lips without a second thought. "I love everything about you and us and how you make me feel. I never want to lose that. Please don't rip my damn heart out. I'm opening up to you, Styx. I'm giving you my all."

"Good." He smiles against my lips and then kisses me hard and deep. "Because I'm a giver when it comes to someone I love and I'm giving you every fucking thing I have in me, beginning with my damn heart."

With that, he slides his jacket off and places it over my shoulders. "Let me get you inside where it's warm."

He wraps his arms around me from behind as I reach for my keys and unlock the door.

As soon as we get inside, he picks me up and begins carrying me through the house, stopping in front of my bed.

"Now I'm spending the rest of the night making love to my woman." He reaches into his pocket and tosses his phone across the room, before laying me down on the bed. "No fucking distractions. Just the two of us."

I smile and then pull him down on top of me, capturing my lips with his.

This man is perfect and I promise to take care of him just as much as he takes care of me . . .

chapter
TWENTY-THREE

STYX

TWO WEEKS LATER . . .

TODAY IS MEADOW'S BIRTHDAY AND all she asked for was some private time for us once we're both done working for the day.

Between spending time with my mother on our days off and working at the gym whenever we both can make it in, we haven't had much of the quiet time that we both enjoy so much.

Today's been an extremely long day for the both of us so I'm desperately waiting for her to make her way back into my damn arms so I can take care of her.

I look down at my phone to see that Meadow should be arriving any second and my heart starts racing with excitement.

This woman manages to make my heart race every damn day that we're together and that's a feeling that I'm not used to. That's how I know just how special she is.

The headlights of her truck shine on the rock that I'm sitting on, letting me know that she's arrived.

Smiling, I stand up and light the single candle on the cupcake, making my way to her as she steps out of her truck looking completely exhausted and worn down.

Her eyes light up the minute she sees what I'm holding. "God, you're the sweetest." She runs at me, throwing her arms around my neck.

I hold the cupcake at a safe distance from her and press my face into her hair and whisper," Happy birthday, baby. I feel like crap that I didn't know until last week. There's a whole batch of these ugly frosted fuckers that I attempted to bake for you at home. Clearly, I need to stick to cooking and not baking."

She cries into my neck where she places a gentle kiss. "It's beautiful. This means so much to me."

When she pulls away from my neck, I dip my thumb into the frosting and then wipe it across her bottom lip. "This looks so much better on you."

I pull her frosted lip into my mouth, sucking off all the blue, before kissing her and then pulling off my leather jacket to drape it over her shoulders.

She laughs and then smashes the cupcake into my mouth, before tossing it aside and kissing me so damn hard that I almost lose my balance.

"This is one of the nicest things anyone has done for me. Why must you keep making me fall for you more and more each day?"

Picking her up, I wrap her legs around my waist and start walking back over to the rock to set her down. "Because you're worth it."

I jump onto the rock behind Meadow, just like the first night I brought her here, pulling her close to me.

My arms wrapped around her.

Her between my thighs.

No words are exchanged.

We just sit here.

Both lost in thought.

Everything else in the world forgotten for the moment as we sit here, staring up at the sky.

Just two people enjoying each other's comfort for a while.

I have a feeling that I'm never going to want to let her go . . .

The End

Read on for a preview of *Kash*
(unedited sample)
Look for the final book in the WOS Series coming early 2017

KASH

chapter ONE

Kash

I SHOW UP AT THE house, to see that Stone, Myles and Colt are already waiting outside for me, dressed in their fitted suits.

Stone tugs on his tie and checks out my hoodie and jeans as if there's something wrong with the way I look.

"Dude . . ." he pushes my hood back. "Where's your suit? I thought we all agreed to dress up and shit. You look like a homeless stripper."

I unzip my hoodie and walk past him with a grin, pulling it open so he can see my ripped up t-shirt. Then I zip it back up when he flicks a rolled up dollar bill at my head.

He knows I said no repeatedly to dressing up, but he ended the call assuming I'd listen anyway. "Nah, you three agreed on a suit. My ass got called out of bed in the middle of the night to be here so I threw on the first thing I saw."

Gotta stand out somehow when it comes to making money

and women like a little mystery.

Myles laughs when Colt looks down at his own suit as if he feels overdressed now.

"I'm making sure this thing comes off fast. I look like an idiot. I told your asses we shouldn't have dressed up."

Walking up to the door, I begin to think we're at the wrong house, because it's completely quiet. No sound of people talking or even a TV playing in the background.

These kinds of parties are always filled with wild women, that can't sit still or wait for us to arrive. There's no way anyone inside that house is waiting on us.

Stone loosens his collar and stands back as if he's checking out the address. "This is it. Just walk in and start shaking your dick. They're probably waiting on us to get the party started."

I'm just about to open the door, when a whistle comes from across the street, making me look over.

"Over here!" Some girl with long, curly blonde hair crosses her arms and leans against the closed door, watching us as we cross the street. "My friend gets confused about her address when she drinks. Either that or she just likes to screw with people. I haven't figured it out yet."

I stop in front of her and take a few moments to check her out in her tight jeans and lose fitting shirt that hangs off one shoulder.

She looks unamused by our arrival as if she's only here because she was forced to be. The concentration on her face as she looks down at her phone and types fast, tells me that there's somewhere else she'd rather be.

"Just go in and start doing whatever it is that you do. The others are eagerly awaiting your arrival. They've been talking dicks all night."

Stone and the newest members of the club, step inside

without hesitation, while I take this moment to breathe in the coolness of the night air and wake up a bit more.

Screams of excitement fill the house, before music blares over the speakers, making it clear that the party has started without me.

"Why aren't you inside with the others? Groping half-naked men isn't your thing?"

She looks up from her phone and gives me a half smile. "Only on some nights."

I laugh at her response and pull out a cigarette, lighting it up. I need to be more awake for this.

Out of the corner of my eye, I notice her checking me out, but I pretend that I don't notice.

"You going to keep that hood up all night? Not quite as handsome as the other guys? Is that it? Don't be shy. I'm sure you have a great body that will do the trick just fine for my friends."

I smile and take a drag of my cigarette, slowly exhaling. As much as she doesn't want to admit it, she's desperate to see what's under this hood and probably even my jeans.

Leaning against the door, I push my hood back and smirk as her eyes wander over my face, doing a double take, before stopping on my lips.

She swallows and then clears her throat, trying to hide the fact that she's surprised by what she sees. "Better get inside with the others. Joni will notice that she paid for four guys and only has three actually earning their pay."

I lift a brow and watch as she pulls the screen door open and disappears inside.

After I finish my cigarette, I pull my hood back up and enter the house.

Walking through the living room, I notice a lot of heads turn my way, eyes watching me as if they can't wait to see what's under this mysterious, black fabric.

One girl even walks away from Myles in an attempt to check me out.

I walk slowly, ignoring them all, letting my eyes seek out the sassy blonde from outside.

She's in the kitchen pouring a drink, but looks over when a few of her friends grab me and pull me back into the living room.

I stand with a confident smile as they start to grab at my hoodie, unzipping it and checking me out as they rip it from my arms.

Hands grope at my chest, lifting at my shirt as I begin to move my hips to Ride by *Chase Rice*.

The sassy blonde smirks from the kitchen, watching the other girls take advantage of me as if she finds it funny.

She's pretending as if she's only watching for the amusement of me being attacked, but the look in her amber eyes gives off the truth of why she hasn't turned away yet.

She wants to see me naked just as badly as they do.

Keeping my eyes on her, I bend one of the girls over, place my hand on her lower back and grind my hips to the rhythm.

I grind slow and seductive, before giving her one hard thrust, almost knocking her over.

She turns back to look at me, her eyes filled with want, before she lays down on her back and waves me over with her finger.

Standing above her, I slowly pull my shirt over my head, before tossing it aside and dropping down to the ground, rolling my body above hers and rubbing my face over her breasts.

Money flies at me as I place her legs over my shoulders and lift her body up, grinding into her, while on my knees.

I gently place her down to her back again, before jumping to my feet and reaching for the closest girl next to me, flipping her upside down so that my cock is grinding against her face.

Slowly turning around with the girl in my arms, I glance into the kitchen to see the sexy little blonde's eyes on me. As soon as our eyes meet, she turns away and goes back to typing on her phone.

Why the fuck does that make me want to get to her even more?

I slap the girl's ass, before flipping her over and setting her back down to her feet.

Cracking my neck, I reach for the button of my jeans, causing desperate screams from all around the room.

I lick my bottom lip, slipping my hand inside my jeans and running it over my erection, while slowly letting my pants fall lower with each move of my hips.

My eyes are still on the sassy blonde in the kitchen when she looks up again to see what I'm doing.

Catching her off guard, I slide across the floor on my knees, grabbing her ass and lifting her up so that her legs are wrapped around my neck.

Her hands grip at my hair for support as I stand to my feet and walk her over to the wall, pressing her back against it.

Moving to the rhythm, I grab her legs and lower her down my body, until her legs are wrapped around my waist now.

She says something that the music drowns out, while I hold her up with my hips, pinning her arms against the wall. I move against her sexy fucking body, while thrusting her up the wall with my erection pressed between her legs.

Fuck, this is extremely hot, making me wish there was nothing between our bodies.

She shows enjoyment for a few short seconds, before dropping her legs to the ground and then pushing at my chest, as I release her arms.

"I'm not here for the entertainment. I'm here for my friend. Find someone else to fuck against the wall."

I stand in the middle of the room sweaty as fuck, trying to catch my breath as I watch her walk out the front door and leave.

One of the girls close by runs her hand over my arm, pulling my attention away from the door. "Don't mind her. Eden spends most of her time at a construction site with dirty men. She forgets what *fun* is sometimes." The brunette grabs my hand and starts pulling me to the other side of the room where a group of women are standing in a circle. "Let's keep this party rocking and rolling, baby. I paid good money for you fine ass men to take your clothes off."

I glance at the door one last time, before looking around me to see the other guys practically naked by this point. All except Stone who refuses to lose his jeans at private parties.

Usually, I'd be having the time of my fucking life, covered in chocolate or whipped cream by now.

But damn . . . this party seems a lot less fun without the fucking sassy blonde watching me.

acknowledgements

FIRST AND FOREMOST, I'D LIKE to say a big thank you to all of my loyal readers that have given me support over the last few years and have encouraged me to continue with my writing. Your words have all inspired me to do what I enjoy and love. Each and every one of you mean a lot to me and I wouldn't be where I am if it weren't for your support and kind words.

I'd also like to thank my beta readers. I love you ladies and appreciate you taking the time to read my words. And SE Hall. Oh my goodness, lady. You helped me more than you can ever know! Thank you so much.

My amazingly, wonderful PA, Amy Preston Rogers. Her support has meant so much to me.

I'd like to thank another friend of mine, Clarise Tan from *CT Cover Creations* for creating my cover. You've been wonderful to work with and have helped me in so many ways.

Thank you to my boyfriend, friends and family for understanding my busy schedule and being there to support me through the hardest part. I know it's hard on everyone, and everyone's support means the world to me.

Last but not least, I'd like to thank all of the wonderful book bloggers that have taken the time to support my book and help spread the word. You all do so much for us authors and it is greatly appreciated. I have met so many friends on the way and you guys are never forgotten. You guys rock. Thank you!

about the author

VICTORIA ASHLEY GREW UP IN Rockford, IL and has had a passion for reading for as long as she can remember. After finding a reading app where it allowed readers to upload their own stories, she gave it a shot and writing became her passion.

She lives for a good romance book with tattooed bad boys that are just highly misunderstood and is not afraid to be caught crying during a good read. When she's not reading or writing about bad boys, you can find her watching her favorite shows such as Supernatural, Sons Of Anarchy, Game Of Thrones and The Walking Dead.

She is the author of Wake Up Call, This Regret, Slade, Hemy, Cale, Stone, Get Off On The Pain, Something For The Pain, Thrust, Royal Savage and is currently working on more works for 2016.

CONTACT HER AT:
www.victoriaashleyauthor.com
Facebook
Twitter: @VictoriaAauthor
Intstagram: VictoriaAshley.Author

books by victoria ashley

WAKE UP CALL
THIS REGRET

SLADE (WALK OF SHAME #1)
HEMY (WALK OF SHAME #2)
CALE (WALK OF SHAME #3)

STONE (WALK OF SHAME 2ND GENERATION #1)

THRUST
GET OFF ON THE PAIN
SOMETHING FOR THE PAIN
ROYAL SAVAGE (SAVAGE & INK #1)

BOOKS CO-WRITTEN WITH HILARY STORM
PAY FOR PLAY (ALPHACHAT.COM SERIES #1)
TWO CAN PLAY (ALPHACHAT.COM SERIES #2)

Made in the USA
Middletown, DE
07 June 2018